FLING *and Other Stories*

JOHN HERSEY

FLING *and Other Stories*

ALFRED A. KNOPF

New York 1990

The short stories in this collection were originally published in the following publications: "God's Typhoon," *The Atlantic*, January, 1988; "Peggety's Parcel of Shortcomings," *The Atlantic*, June, 1950; "Fling," *Grand Street*, Summer, 1987; "The Blouse," *Special Report: Fiction*, May–July, 1989; "The Announcement," *The Atlantic*, October, 1989; "Why Were You Sent Out Here?," *The Atlantic*, February, 1947; "Requiescat," *Paris Review*, No. 107, Summer, 1988; "The Captain," *The Yacht*, November/December, 1988; "Mr. Quintillian," *The Yale Review*, Fall, 1987; "The Terrorist," *Esquire*, August, 1987; "Affinities," *Shenandoah*, Vol. XXXVII-2, 1987.

ISBN 0-394-58338-0
LC 89-43352

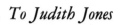

To Judith Jones

"Tongue, whither wilt thou?" says the old proverb.
"I go to build," says the Tongue, *"and I go to pull down."*

FROM *The Life of Aesop*,
BY SIR ROGER L'ESTRANGE,
LONDON, 1694.

CONTENTS

FLING *and Other Stories*

God's Typhoon

In the lot next to ours at the summer resort of Peitaiho, at the foot of the hill that swooped down toward Rocky Point and the "American beach" and the sparkling North China Sea, Dr. Wyman had planted his famous arboretum. It boasted every conifer that could survive in that slice of the temperate zone. I was a small boy; I didn't know the names of any of the trees, but I was in awe of the grove. I did not dare go into it. Even Dr. Wyman's three sons had been strictly ordered to stay out. Huge NO TRESPASSING signs, in English and Chinese, capped its shoulder-high stone walls. Only Dr. Wyman and his invited guests, who were few and far between, were allowed entry—besides, of course, Chinese coolies to tend the grounds.

On days when I was bored, I used to sit on a boulder in our lot and contemplate that exquisite little forest. Salty sea breezes off the Gulf of Peichili had gnarled many of the pines and firs and spruces and cedars and yews and had caused all their feather-bearing boles to tend to the west, toward the plains and mountains beyond the hill, as if they yearned for the bone-dry air that sometimes came all the way down from the Gobi Desert. On foggy days even I could sense something of the mystery in evergreen shapes that had entranced so many Chinese painter-philosophers. Through the years the trees had woven a brownish-green carpet on the ground, and after a rain a delicious fragrance of resin and sweet gum spilled over onto our land.

Quite often I saw Dr. Wyman strolling alone along the paths among the trees, with his head thrown back as if to drink. Sometimes I saw his mouth moving. Possibly he was rehearsing his dreadful sermons.

His son Billy Wyman and I both had brothers who were old enough to be Boy Scouts, while we two were still only Wolf Cubs. North China reverberated that summer with the cannon fire of warlords' battles, and the Scouts were constantly being mobilized, in their insufferable (to us) uniforms with red kerchiefs and merit badges all up and down their arms and chests, to run errands for the 15th U.S. Infantry and the Royal Marines. Those troops were bivouacked to protect foreign persons and their property at this heavenly enclave on Chinese soil, where Chinese persons—except, naturally, for house servants and coolies and donkey tenders—were unwelcome.

Furious at being kept at home under our mothers' wings while the big boys were out defending us, Billy and I spent every minute we could in and around a pup tent, defending an imaginary world of our own. I played soldier and he, being a Brit, played marine. Our good guy was the warlord Wu Pei-fu, our sworn enemy the Japanese-supported Chang Tso-lin. We were very brave but not brave enough to pitch our tent near Billy's house. We were both scared of his father.

The Reverend Doctor Josephus P. Wyman had remarkable gifts of body and mind. He seemed as tall and broad and dangerous, coming along one of the resort's sandy roads, as a lorry, and when he ground his jaws in a grimace of effort, as he often did, his chin and throat muscles bulged so much that you expected a bullfrog's song to come out from between his huge, pipesmoke-tinted teeth. Billy said he had once scored six hundred and seventeen runs at one stretch as a cricketer for Oxford. His interminable sermons at the Union Church came at us in an insistent singsong, half whine, half roar, and my restlessness in the pews on those Sabbath mornings was edged with dread.

Dr. Wyman preached a God I couldn't quite see in my mind, and certainly couldn't love. I dimly pictured some kind of Grandfather, who dealt out to bad people their awful "just deserts," which I thought must be poisoned food at the end of delicious meals. Grandfathers seemed mysterious and rather awesome to me anyhow, because I had never seen my two, both of whom lived back in the States. The Grandfather Dr. Wyman talked about was suspicious and angry, for no reason I could perceive. Shouldn't He be wildly happy over having created, among other wondrous things, our ravishing summer resort? Yet this Grandfather apparently spent most of His time on the lookout for ways of punishing everybody's "trespasses" and "sins of pride." Dr. Wyman harped on sins of pride. After his sermons I gloomily wondered about mine. Something to do with merit badges? Skill in swimming the Australian crawl?

Dr. Wyman was a polymath; we could imagine no subject on which he could not bury an adversary under the ever-spreading lava of his knowledge. His house—a queer, ugly block of stone with a flat roof, which he had designed him-self—was like an untidy museum, crammed with all sorts of tools and instruments invented by man in order to assist in the study of God's manifest ingenuities. Strewn about on work-benches, parlor chairs, the dining-room table, and even his poor wife's sewing machine and ironing board, were Bunsen burners, microscopes, several of the latest cameras, a delicate balance with tiny scalepans, a stereoscope, numerous magnifying glasses, racks of test tubes holding various ominous-looking fluids; scattered here and there were sets of pipettes and syringes and beakers, of scalpels and chisels and dissecting knives, slide rules and compasses and tape measures, electromagnets and inductor coils and Leyden jars. Only Dr. Wyman's Deity knew what else—but oh! also a crystal radio capable of picking up Peking, a telegraph key on which he had conversed in Morse code with Vladivostok, and, most majestic of all, right in the center of the parlor, causing some awkwardness in group conversation there, a seven-foot-long telescope that he sometimes lugged up onto the roof at night to make sure the spheres were still revolving in God's good order.

Though known for his brilliance, he was also a jovial man. My mother had said that his laughter was as loud as the roar of Niagara Falls. Adults agreed that he was conscientious and tender in his pastoral duties; he was wonderfully sweet to Mrs. Fenton, they said, a cranky old lady, whom Billy and I used to mimic, sitting on her veranda all day in a rocking chair, moaning. I had heard Billy's mother say that breathing the piny air in the arboretum was what made the Reverend, as she called him, so serene.

Yet I was afraid of him. The reason for this—beyond whatever it was in his marathon sermons that set my nerves twanging—was the kind of boy his son, my friend Billy, was turning out to be. Pale, thin, washed-out, obedient, with eyes as sad as those of a bloodhound, Billy wore shorts that hung down below his knees, and scuffed black shoes with no socks. He made a hopeless Royal Marine. He was a wonderful pal to have, though, because he would do anything I asked him to. But I pitied him, too, and blamed his flaccid condition entirely on his father. If Dr. Wyman could spend so much on a swarm of coolies to tend his conifers, why couldn't he buy Billy some decent clothes, instead of making him wear his older brothers' worn-out hand-me-downs? Couldn't he expend some of his renowned gentleness on his forlorn son? What I saw flicker in Billy's eyes whenever we came roistering into that cluttered house and found Dr. Wyman looming there over some foul-smelling chemicals in an experiment he was touchily conducting—the pain I glimpsed in Billy's eyes at such a moment—told me that he was mortally afraid of that big, kind man.

One day I had a thrilling idea: Billy and I would camp out overnight in the pup tent. I asked my mother if we could. "You'll have to ask your father," she said.

I waited until after he had won a tennis match, six–one, six–love, and then I did.

"Do you have your mother's permission?" he asked me.

"I haven't had a chance to check with her," I said.

"Come back when you have her permission," he said.

This was a game of shuttle diplomacy at which I had become adept, and before long I had my go-ahead. I announced the plan to Billy. He shook his head back and forth only about a quarter of an inch each way—an economical gesture that expressed an enormous negative. He would never get permission from his father. I suggested that, to begin with, we go to work on his mother.

Mrs. Wyman seemed at first glance to be one of those deeply wounded but resigned ladies—of whom there were so very many among missionary wives—who wore shapeless dresses and were always having to push back, with a sigh, stubborn stray tresses of their prematurely gray hair and refasten them any which way with one of a shoal of tortoiseshell hairpins. She had no territory of her own in her home. Dr. Wyman had considerately set aside a small oaken desk on which she might keep his accounts, but he had ruined its surface by spilling some acid during one of his explorations of God's marvelous secrets. Yet with my shrewd small-boy's eyes I had often observed the way she could balance the huge minister on the little finger of her left hand while her right hand was doing something that would have astonished if not outraged him, had he but noticed. She had Scottish blood and a residue of lake-country canniness in her makeup.

The long and the short of it was that we got permission from Wyman *mère* and later, with *mère*'s help but not without growls, from *père*. Protocols drawn up by Dr. Wyman required that the tent be pitched no more than twenty feet from the sleeping porch of our house, so that, if necessary, a yell would waken my parents. We were not to stir from inside the tent after sunset and before dawn. We could not sleep in our clothes but would have to wear pajamas. No foodstuffs, no matches, no loud talk.

It was dark in the tent, and we obeyed all the rules that first night.

For a while, the warlords having packed themselves off, Billy and I had to try to keep up with the energies of our older brothers. We galloped to East Cliff on donkeyback, left far behind by the big boys, in a paper chase—a simulated fox hunt, introduced at Peitaiho by British missionaries, in which the hunters followed a trail of torn-up bits of back issues of *The Peking and Tientsin Times*, which had been scattered earlier for miles across the country by an adult "master of hounds." We fished for puffers from Tiger Rocks, off the American beach, and under the pressure of dares from the bigger boys we dived in terror into mysterious boulder-rimmed depths off the high "forehead rock." They made us serve as ball boys for their tennis tournament, and allowed us to shag foul balls when they played baseball against the 15th Infantry team, which always beat the missionary kids by scores like 33–2, in five innings.

On some days our brothers refused to let "the brats" tag along, and we went howling to our mothers. A few of those days turned out to be the sweetest of the summer. Once, taking pity on us, Mrs. Wyman sent her Number One Boy down to the village to find an itinerant rice-paste sculptor, who came up the hill carrying the two cylindrical cases of his "studio" on a shoulder pole; in twenty minutes, for two coppers, mixing and tinting and molding the plasticene-like paste, he made for Billy and me a pair, each eight inches tall, of magnificently ferocious warriors of the era of the Three Kingdoms. The next time was my mother's turn, and she sent our Wang down to find a magician, who, also with his gear in two containers on a shoulder pole, dazzled us on our front veranda, pulling silk cloths out of his ear, and asking Billy and me to try to guess which shifting riceware cup the jade grasshopper was under, and even finding a live dove in my mother's hat, the one with red wax cherries on it, which she had left lying on the glider that day. Once we were entertained by child acrobats. Once we were allowed to make ice cream in midafternoon in the hand-turned freezer, with rock-salted ice, both of us licking the mixing blade at the same time.

The greatest treat of all for me—we had learned to redouble our howls when the big boys left us behind—was the day Dr. Wyman took us for a walk in the arboretum. My fear of him vanished, and I was glad to have him keep hold of my hand along the cavernous, deep-shaded paths. Birds were in ecstasy among the slivers of light overhead. The needle scent acted on me like opium, and I felt that I was floating, to the music of the Latin names of species that Dr. Wyman softly recited, in a kind of dream I had never even hoped to have.

A few days later news came that troops of Chang Tso-lin had shown up again near Shanhaikwan, only a few miles from us, where the Great Wall came down to the sea. The big boys were called up for guard duty, and Billy and I wheedled and whined until we were given permission to sleep out in the tent another time.

It was a full-moon night. The cloth of the tent glowed. I

could not sleep. I don't know what time it was when something perverse surged up in me and I whispered, "Billy?"

He, too, was wide awake. "What?"

"Let's go down to the arboretum."

"*Now?*"

"Sure. It's a wizard night."

"It's against the rules," Billy said.

"Pshaw, Billy"—the closest I could come to swearing at that time—"don't be a spoilsport."

"I don't think Daddy would like it."

But Billy would do anything I asked him to, and soon we were two bright ghosts in our white PJs, slinking downhill along the three-foot-high border wall of my family's lot, both of us in a crouch, as if that would hide us from the searching light of the moon. The gate to the arboretum was locked. I had to help Billy up onto the wall and then, my heart beating wildly, I jumped up after him. We sat there on the curved plaster top quite a while, not daring to hurry down the other side. Finally I scrambled down. Billy still hesitated. I tugged at him, until finally his need for compliance overcame his fear, and he slithered down.

When our eyes had adjusted to the shadows, we started along the central path. I held Billy's hand. I had goose pimples all up and down my back and arms and legs. We did not speak.

Somewhere far away—not in the grove, I am now convinced—an owl suddenly hooted, and Billy and I turned and ran. He got over the wall this time without any help.

A British submarine cruised like a shark on the surface of the silver gulf and anchored in our bay, close enough to shore that boys even as small as Billy and I could swim out—nervous all the way—to look it over. Its presence lent a new naval arm to our daytime military operations in and around the pup tent. Since nothing naughty or dangerous appeared to have happened, our sleeping out in the tent on fair-weather nights had now come to be accepted by both mothers—and therefore had been sanctioned with doubtful glowers by the supposed final authorities, the fathers. The next three times after our adventure in the arboretum, we pitched the tent at sundown, crawled in, and more or less scrupulously followed the rules. But as I lay awake on the hard ground on those nights, something kept gnawing at me, filling me with delight and fear.

Finally, one afternoon, on the most delicious day of the summer, with a sky like the inside of a beautiful seedless Concord grape and air so calm that time seemed to have stopped, I waited until we were in a good mood after having routed Chang Tso-lin for the hundredth time, and then I said to Billy, "Tell you what, let's do something big."

"Oh, no," Billy said, the blood fleeing from his cheeks. "What now?"

I grabbed him by the shirt and whispered, "Tonight, after everyone's asleep, we'll strike the tent and take it down to the arboretum and pitch it in, you know, that open clearing. And sleep there. Wouldn't that be neat?"

Billy looked as if I had stabbed him. I kept whispering. I told him I'd take my new little alarm clock with us; we could get up at five and bring the tent back up, and no one would ever know. It would be easy. Sleeping so near the house had gotten boring.

"It's so dark down there," Billy said.

"I've thought about that," I said. "Listen, Billy, you know that coal miner's hat of your father's, the one with the little kerosene lamp fastened to it over the visor? I've noticed it's in that jumbled heap of stuff in the corner of your what-do-you-call-it, spare room?—where he just throws junk—you know?—that he's never going to use again? That he's completely forgotten about? We could borrow that."

I was pushing Billy into the very pith of danger, and I knew it. And I know now that this awareness was the knife-edge of my excitement. Another thing I knew then was that Billy would in time come round to doing what I asked. It took a lot of whispering, but Billy came round.

It was about eleven o'clock, and the lights had long been out in both our houses, when we surreptitiously pulled up the tent pegs and collapsed the poles and folded the canvas. I had sneaked a tin of wick oil out to the tent and had filled the miner's lamp, and I had a box of wooden matches in the pocket of my shorts. (A couple of tent-nights ago we had given up changing into pajamas, though each time we would bundle them up and use them as pillows, so that our mothers could see the next day that they were wrinkled and soiled.) Of course we would wait until later to light the lamp, but I put the hat on Billy's head. There was a dim glow from a gibbous moon high in the sky. I looked up at it and shivered. It had a strange misty ring around it. It was like an eye in the sky, looking right at us. It knew everything. It must have been able to make out, as I could in its cold glare, that the miner's hat was too big for Billy's head but that it somehow stayed in place. He was going to be the one to wear it.

When we got the tent over the wall and had gone over ourselves, I lit the lamp. It created a magical sphere of soft visibility, into the fuzzy outer membrane of which, as we stole toward the glade, all the varieties of evergreens reached their feathery hands to greet us. I felt blissful, and even Billy was moved; he said in a trembling voice, "Say, this is keen." We pitched the tent with no trouble, crept in, snuffed the lamp, and bedded down on the fragrant carpet. We whispered awhile, but soon I drifted off into the deepest sleep I'd ever had on this earth.

I was having a frightful dream. The entire tent was snatched away from over us in a sudden swoop, like a single beat of the wings of a huge condor, and I heard a deep roaring, as of some great natural cataclysm. But no, no, I wasn't dreaming, I was all too awake. I sat up, my buttocks aprickle, and I sensed that Billy was sitting up beside me, whimpering. Dr. Wyman stood over us, glowing in the moonlight in his pajamas. The words of his rage broke on me like rough waves roiling me in the sand. With a grip on the ridgepole, he held the whole tent high in his right hand. "Up! Up!" he shouted. "Pick up your things!" he roared. As we scrambled about, he saw the miner's hat. "You brought a flame into my arboretum," he said in a kind of groan. "You lit matches under these trees." Then he leaned his huge face down toward me and shouted twice, "You little devil! You little devil!"

In my bed on our sleeping porch, much, much later, I could still hear, all the way from the Wymans' house, Billy crying out till I thought his lungs must burst.

The next afternoon I could only imagine that Mrs. Wyman felt her youngest duckling had been too severely punished in the night, and that she had begged the Reverend in the morning for Christian forgiveness. Because, to my astonishment, Billy was allowed to come over to play with me. The rims of his eyes were purple. I was sincere in my apologies to him and promised I would never get him in trouble again, and he, with his gentle, fragile nature, forgave me. But our play around the tent, which we repitched in its "safe" place twenty feet from our sleeping porch, was halfhearted. I didn't feel like singing out commands to Billy with my usual bravura. The day was sticky, and depressing. Despite a lack of wind on our cheeks, swift clouds scudded in from the sea, low overhead. We perspired. Chang Tso-lin languished in the enemy camp. I kept thinking that although Dr. Wyman had leaned down and spoken those last few words to me in sermon tones the night before, he must surely have meant the word "devil" only in a slangy sort of way, to be written in my heavenly record with a lowercase initial. Not the real thing. I sniffed my arm and could not smell burning sulfur. Billy was sympathetic. He saw how bad I felt, and to cheer me up he kept making suggestions: we could send a scouting party around the other side of the house, we could radio the sub to search toward Lighthouse Point. . . .

Later I was in the tent. "Hey," Billy said, "come out here."

I knew the various timbres of his voice, and I heard a ring in this summons that made me scramble out pell-mell on my hands and knees.

"Look," he said, pointing out to the gulf.

Above the horizon, along its whole span, rolled a cloud as black as charcoal, with a sickish viridian light between it and the sea, and then I saw what had alarmed Billy, as if the endless cloud itself weren't bad enough. On a bearing straight out from the submarine there hung down from the black cloud a slender conical tendril, equally black, which seemed at first to weave slightly back and forth. Then it grew longer, like a finger poking down, down. Next, in horror, as if we, too young, were watching a primal scene of unspeakable obscenity, sea mating with sky, we saw a cone rise up from the water and move in a wavering way toward the shore, dancing in response to the finger above, separate from it but following directly beneath it. With a sudden spurt, vapor and water flew together, and the sky began to suck up the sea.

Now we realized that the sinuous spout was coming close to the shore. Miraculously it took a detour around the submarine, which lay calmly at anchor at the rim of the vortex of violent whitecaps surrounding the column. I heard my mother screaming my name. The twister reached land, half a mile from us, and Billy and I saw a cottage seem to explode. Its roof—all the foreigners' cottages at Peitaiho had corrugated tin roofs—was ripped off in pieces, and huge sheets of metal and scraps of wood and branches of trees and a million fragments of everything rose and revolved and fell, until another house was hit, and after that . . . but Billy and I turned away and ran for it. My mother hugged me, and my father shouted, "You boys hold the sleeping-porch door shut!" We two, glad to have work to do, ran to that door, which, though it was latched, was already trembling. We braced ourselves against it. I was thinking how glad I was not to be able to see what was happening outside, when with a splitting sound the jamb gave way and the door flew open, throwing Billy and me to the floor halfway across the room. On hands and knees in the indoor gale, I looked up and saw the roof of the McAlisters' house, beyond and to the left of the Wymans', lifted off whole, almost exactly as the pup tent had been ripped from above us the night before, and I heard a roar that sounded to me just like Dr. Wyman's rage. The typhoon was calling me names. I closed my eyes. I heard a terrible crash but felt no pain. Then the ministerial roar seemed to move on toward other devils in other houses. The wind suddenly died. Torrents of water came down as the sky's buckets of salt sea fell back on us. Our house had held.

An hour after the wind subsided, but while it was still pouring, my oldest brother, Peter, the most adventurous of the three of us boys, rushed out of the house to scout the wreckage on our Rocky Point hill. My mother called to him to come back, but he ran on. He had not gone far when he noticed a knot of people in the Wymans' lot, and he ran to them and saw that they were standing in a soaked circle around Dr. Wyman's dead body. Of course Peter rushed back to tell us about it. He used to boast about the accuracy of his observations, and he described the cadaver to us in gruesome detail. A huge sheet of metal from the McAlisters' roof, skimming along over the ground "at a hundred miles an hour," Peter said, had cut Dr. Wyman in two at the waist and then had flipped away, leaving the two halves of the pastor prone in what still seemed to be something like a running position. The driving rain had washed away all the blood.

"And, oh, by the way," Peter said, "every single tree in the arboretum was uprooted. You should see the mess—trunks in all directions. It's a rat's nest."

Hearing these things, I experienced a surge of the greatest joy I had ever known. The Grandfather in Heaven was, after all, capable of love, and He loved me. He had brought this typhoon for me. The roar of the storm's rage had not been meant for me at all; it had been aimed at Billy's father. This God whom I welcomed at last was both merciful and angry, for He had forgiven me my trespasses and punished Dr. Wyman for his. I was sorry, deeply sorry, about the arboretum, but it seemed to me that in destroying it, God may have been pointing a finger at one of Dr. Wyman's sins of pride. From my Sunday-school lore I conjured up a dim sense that Dr. Wyman had tried to create—with only his coolies' help, not God's—a Garden of Eden of his own, which he had wanted to keep forever for Adam's own selfish use.

My joy, my conversion, my perfect faith, lasted only a day. The next morning, though the downpour was by no means over, my other brother, Amos, went across to the Wymans' house, and when he came back, he told me he'd heard Mrs. Wyman say that the reason the Reverend had been out there in the fury of the storm was that he had gone to look for Billy, to rescue him from danger. That changed everything. I began to have nightmares every night.

We had three solid days of torrential rain. Miraculously, our house had suffered only minor damage. A six-foot-square piece of roofing had struck our porch roof—the crash I had heard. The skirts of the twister must have swerved just enough to miss us; the McAlisters' house in one direction and two on the other side of us were hit hard. Dr. Wyman's little storm-proof box had taken the full force of the wind, with no damage but some broken windows. A few days later Amos found the canvas of the pup tent undamaged in a sorghum field a quarter of a mile from the house. The ridgepole was still in it but was broken; we never found the uprights.

I didn't see Billy for a fortnight. Because of the bad dreams I was having, my mother thought I should probably not go to the funeral. (After it, I overheard her scolding Peter for having told us all a fib the day of the storm: she had learned that Dr. Wyman had not been cut in two at all, though he had indeed been mortally wounded at the midriff.) The weather turned lovely. Our Number One Boy, Wang, was a clever carpenter, and he liked me; he made new poles and pegs for the tent, and I finally set it up in the "safe" place, but I had no fun playing around it alone.

The very next day Billy came over. I hardly recognized him. He had on brand-new white shorts, I could see his nubby knees, and he was wearing Keds. His hair was brushed. When we started our war game, he had some rather impertinent suggestions—they proved to be good ones, I had to admit— about maneuvers against Chang Tso-lin.

Before he left for home, he said, "Let's sleep in the arboretum tonight."

I was astonished at his taking that kind of initiative. "Gee, Billy," I said, "it's a ruin."

"I know," he said. "It belongs to me now. My brothers aren't interested. Mama said I could replant it."

"Replant it? What are you going to use for seeds?"

"Daddy has—I mean he had—masses of seeds. And I've already sent for some seedlings from Szechuan. One of the China Inland Missions advertises them in the *Recorder*, you know—jolly good cedars just like those in the Holy Land."

I slept poorly that night in what had been the clearing in the arboretum. Billy snored. In the morning he boiled water on a Sterno rack that he had brought in his knapsack, and made tea for us. Dr. Wyman's squad of coolies showed up with two-man saws. Billy had the key to the gate and let them in, and he told them where to start cutting up the trunks. He said he was going to try to right some of the very young trees, which still seemed to have life in them, and he asked me to help him with one of the smaller ones. He grabbed hold of the trunk with me and began straining, and I saw that his teeth were clenched and his pathetic jaw muscles and neck muscles were all tightened up.

Peggety's Parcel
of Shortcomings

"I well remember," said Miss Peg, the pastry cook, with a coffee éclair hovering in her fingers, "the night I fell into the embrace of the United States Merchant Marine. I weighed scant two hundred eight pounds at that time. I was, you might say, thin as a shelf."

Probably Miss Peg meant to say "sylph." In fairness, you had to grant to Miss Peg that she was always willing to risk elegance, if there was any of it handy. Only sometimes her tongue slipped—especially if it was all lubricated to receive an éclair or a napoleon.

They were gathered—Miss Peg, Mrs. Manterbaum, and Johnny the second busboy—in the pantry locker down in the basement. As pastry chef, Miss Peg kept the key to the locker, and late each evening, about eleven o'clock, when the clubhouse was quite deserted and lay black and junky on the Florida beach, like a tremendous shipwreck, she would ghost in through the service entrance to the basement with one or two guests, unlock the wire mesh door to her locker, light up the single bare bulb that hung down from the ceiling, get out a few good things, seat the party on the wooden crates she kept her pans in, and then she would begin to talk. Mrs. Manterbaum, whose job was to keep the cabañas clean, was notorious among the help for her sweet tooth, a regular sugar-thief, and she had worked herself into the position of being invited by Miss Peg almost every night to taste a few "extra" pastries. Miss Peg used to ask Johnny the second busboy about once a week, because he was good-natured about pushing her pastry cart around to the Big People in the dining room for her. If there was one thing she hated in life, it was cart-pushing. That, and bending down to slide her pans in and out of her ovens.

"I was twenty-three," Miss Peg said, "and I was then doing scullery for a certain Mrs. Charles Saunders in Old Bridge Harbor, on Long Island. Mr. Saunders was in asphalt and, as we used to say, he couldn't get out. Though in truth he was prosperous. Mrs. Saunders had seven in help. I remember one thing about Mr. Saunders, which was, he was very particular about the way his shoes were laid out in the mornings—the laces had to be real loose and the tongues lifted out and bent forward, so he could more or less walk right into his shoes. If Mr. Saunders had any difficulty about walking into his shoes, any morning, he was liable to a very bad state of mind at breakfast, and goodness knew who would feel the shock of it. You understand, I only heard these things. Small Peggety, as they called me—the 'Small' was belittling, you might say, considering my heft—never advanced beyond the Near Pantry, and had no occasion to see Mr. Saunders standing in his own shoes, laced or unlaced. Fact is, the first time I ever laid eyes on him, close by, was the day the United States Merchant Marine and I had our little heave-to.

"It happened in the following particulars. My cousin Bob, who never came across with the rest of us, lives some short distance outside Greenock, by Glasgow, and he being a familiar of certain public houses on the waterfront, travels, you might say, victoriously—by talking with those who go to sea."

"Vicariously," Johnny said.

"I beg your pardon?" Miss Peg said, very grand.

Johnny realized one of the reasons Miss Peg liked him was that he had gone through third year high school and was, in her words, "a bookish lad"; he did read a good bit. Miss Peg had never had any schooling, and her elegance had been picked up over the years of service while she was passing the peas, so to speak. Johnny dared, now and then, to catch her up on some of her errors of overreaching.

"Your cousin Bob," Johnny said, "travels vicariously."

"*Well?*" said Miss Peg, with rising tone, as if to ask why the young scoundrel felt it necessary to repeat something that had already been said. "So one evening," she went on, "Bob met this tidy, small-boned Yank, a Boatswain's Mate, Third Class, in the United States Merchant Marine, named Bufano. A swarthy sort. Talking of one big thing and another, they landed at last upon me, so it was necessary—Bob thought— to tell the fellow all about me. I will say, Bob has a straight tongue, he did not dangle any pretty marionette before this Bufano's eyes. To be blunt about it, he said his cousin Peggety was *fat*. 'So much the better,' says this Bufano. 'I always was squeamish about getting myself bruised against sharp and knobby things. I am glad to hear that you have a nice soft cousin.'

"The first thing *I* knew," said Peg, "I received a postcard written in a fine Eyetalian hand, all curlicues and scrolls on the capital letters, like a birthday cake, saying, '*Meet me outside Ritz corner 46 and Mad six pm Thursday evening. Assume this is helps night out. I have grand news of your cousin Bob from other side. Bufano, Bsns Mate 3/c, S.S. Parton.*' This 'grand news,' " Miss Peg said, leaping ahead in her narrative, as she sometimes did, "was that our Bob was spending much time in the public houses and was a two-hump camel when it came to the ale; he could drink twice as much and hold it twice as long as anyone else. 'Grand news'!

. . .

"The next Thursday," Miss Peg resumed, "I got myself all frilled up, smelling like a church on Easter morning, and Mason the chauffeur was just about to drive the help to the station, and me, sitting there, taking up half the back seat of the car, happy as a lintie thinking about my unknown sailor boy, when out from the quarters comes a message: 'Tell Small Peggety to stop by at Mr. Saunders' office, 30 Rockefeller Plaza. He has a wee errand for her.'

"Our Maggie, the cook, who if I was overweight she was a dried-up apricot of the fuzzy variety, said sarcastic, 'Write down the address. Our Peggety is in love, she's a bag of daydreams, she'll never remember.'

"Between the message and Maggie, it took quite some time for the others to dill me down to where I was calm again. Wasn't it just like Mr. Saunders to save his 'wee errands' for *that* day? Any other time, this command would have made me tingle with the fun of doing it—'thistles in me thumbs,' as our mum used to say when she had a thrill. But that day, it was all I could do to think of my seafaring man with the handwriting like Queen Victoria's Golden Jubilee fireworks.

"Nevertheless, when we reached the city, I went of course as directed to 30 Rockefeller Plaza and I shot up into the sky where Mr. Saunders did his work and up I went to the lady at the desk and I said, trying to be sort of saucy and mature, 'I am the Peggety. Mr. Saunders has a wee errand for me.'

"The lady looked at me and said, 'Sister, aren't you kind of dressed up for *this* errand?'

"So I replied, 'The nature of the work was not divulged, you might say.'

"The lady flicked a switch on a box, and I heard Mr. Saunders' voice come out of the box, only his voice sounded like his nose had been snipped off by a crow or was pinched with a clothespin; he said, 'What is it?'

" 'Your maid,' the lady said into the box, 'has come for the carcass.'

"This gave me the goose pimples all over, and since I was a thimber sort of girl, a large skin area, you might say, there was a considerable amount of puckering up to be got done with.

"Mr. Saunders kind of laughed a noseless laugh from the box and said, 'Send her in.'

"I walked into the office whither the lady nodded, and there he was, the master, looking very wild, but with his nose, thank the Lord, quite unharmed. It must have been merely the mechanics of the box that had taken away his nose from his voice. In general the master was very wild, however. He was in his shirtsleeves and he was dressed in a big white apron and he had in his hand a butcher's knife of the largest sort, and I thought: Oh me, I thought asphalt was used to pave the roads, what *can* it be that the master does for a living?

"He said to me, 'Sit down, girl, I'll be ready in a few minutes.'

"It was then," Miss Peg said, "that I noticed another gentleman in the room, he was dressed in ordinary business clothes, though his look was rather ferocious, too, it seemed to me, but at the time, you must remember, I was only Small Peggety, twenty-three winters along, tipping the scales approximately two-o-eight, with no experience of the world beyond the Near Pantry, consequently this fierceness may have been imaginary on my part.

"I also noticed—and this hit me all of a sudden, like the sun coming out from under a cloud—a smell in the place like Fulton Street at the East River, in other words, fish in all its glory. And by following my senses, I tracked this scent to Mr. Saunders' desk, where lay, about as big as my upper arm, no, bigger yet, a whole salmon. A very substantial fish, I can assure you, Mrs. Manterbaum.

"Mr. Saunders grasped the butcher knife in both hands, and

he began to stagger and struggle around the room, talking the while like that raddio fellow, Mr. Clem McCarthy, dealing with the Derby, in case you are interested in the horses, Mrs. Manterbaum—breathless he was and yet in command of the telling. I soon puzzled it out that Mr. Saunders was describing to his friend the capture of this particular salmon of his. He was using the butcher knife for his rod and reel, and I was fearful lest he would fish himself into total blindness with that sharp thing. And so we had game-fishing all up and down the office for the next half hour. They say that salmon do go upriver in order to make love, and to hear Mr. Saunders speak of the reluctance of this whopper to leave the headwaters of the Skampawam, or whatever the river would be named, in Nova Scotia, it was—to hear *him*, I believe this fish must have been engaged in the romance of the century in the salmon world. Really, the aquarium should be told about it. Well! I tell you! We *finally* landed the thing, but we were panting and giving off a deal of perspiration over it—and there the lecherous rascal was, big as life and ten times smellier, right on Mr. Saunders' desk, asphalt be damned.

" 'He's been thawing out all day,' Mr. Saunders said. 'We shipped him down in dry ice. His guts were cleaned up there, and now'—advancing on the salmon with the dreadful knife, he said this—'now I'm going to lop off his head and tail so the girl here can manage him by hand and take him out home for us, and tomorrow night, Spencer, tomorrow *night*! Well, you'll just have to wait and taste him.'

"Our creature was thawed out, all right, and he gave up his head till there was salmon blood all over the newspapers on Mr. Saunders' desk. Likewise the tail, a smaller operation but also not without splashes and clots of red. By this time the odor of fish was almost a fog around us that you could see. Whew!

"More newspapers, a bundle, string; there we were. 'Now,

girl,' said Mr. Saunders, who, never having been on *my* side
of the Near Pantry, of course did not know me by name, 'now,
girl, you may take it home. And have a care!'

"What a care I had, all that suffering night! And yet . . .

"It was now, you see, pushing six o'clock, because of the
length of Mr. Saunders' description of his triumph over the
poor hooked thing. Thus, if I was to meet my friend with the
birthday-cake handwriting, I would have to rush right over
there, with no time to park my bundle meanwhile. Right
through the newspaper, through goodness knows how many
layers of current events, you could not fail to smell my pink
beheaded treat. Trembling, I dashed to the Ritz, corner of
Madison and Forty-sixth.

"I was on time but early. The Merchant Marine, being a
man of the world, had decided to have a wee tease of Small
Peggety, who knew nothing. So there I stood, before the most
swoshy hotel in the land, waiting, with ladies going by in
ermine and sapphires and curls right out of the permanent-
wave machine, and me, under the marquee with all its sweet
little light bulbs, me, embracing a two-and-a-half-foot stink.
I was mortified to death, Mrs. Manterbaum.

"At last he came and worth waiting for. Short, stocky, and
sort of sunny-Italy-complected. His pants as tight as wedding
gloves. He was a lovely, tiny creature. He strolled right up
to me, with all the swagger of his cute bowlegs, and he said,
raising his white cap, 'Miss Peggety, if I am not mistaken. I
could have spotted you, my dear, from a mile away.'

"Well, he had my heart right then and there, though now
in my calmer years I can see that his first remark—about
kenning me from such a very impressive distance—left something to be desired as a compliment.

"Right there on the street corner, as he gazed up into my

eyes, looking for my soul, you might say, and my heart like a moth by a sixty-watt lamp, I saw that the flanges of his nostrils were working away quite passionate, exactly like Mr. Rudolph Valentino's, but then I realized that it wasn't so much love at first sight as it was he had caught a whiff of something about my person. What he smelt, you already know, Mrs. Manterbaum.

"I had no doubt, in the next moments, that my Bufano was as packed full of gentility as his bell-bottoms were packed full of Bufano. Because without so much as muttering, 'Hm, fishy out tonight, ain't it, Miss Peggety?'—with no such remarks, without a flicker of his lovely waxen eyelids, without even moving to windward of me, he said, 'Well, my dear, what'll it be? Shall we dance? Or is food your pleasure? A steak, Miss Peggety?' You see how well-bred he was? Steak! Any lesser man would have asked me if I was in the mood for a bite of seafood.

"Timid, I said, 'First off, Mr. Bufano, I'd like to run down to Grand Central and check this parcel for the evening.'

"I could see from the way my Bufano looked at the package in my arms that he knew what I was carrying. Jaunty as you please, he swung around and offered me the crook of his arm.

"At the checking place in Grand Central, I just pushed the package across the brass-plated counter. The man there pulled it toward him and actually snapped the checking tag onto the string. Then (I guess his nose was tuned in by this time) he looked up and said, 'What's in here?'

" 'Just some laundry,' I said. My Bufano stiffened a little at that. The counterman thumped at the package with his fists, shook his head, unsnapped the tag, and shoved the thing back to me.

" 'Sorry, lady,' the counterman said, 'we ain't allowed to accept no carrion here.'

"I guess my feelings took a tumble that you could see and

hear, because Bufano said, 'Cheer up, my dear, we'll just hurry over to Pennsylvania Station. We should have done that in the first place. You'll have to leave from there when our spree is over.'

"But the man in the parcel room at Penn Station was even quicker than our Grand Central fellow. Indeed, he looked at us at first with a dread look of suspicion, as if we were trying to dispose of the parts of a human body, one by one. I must confess, with the moisture and even some of the tint of corpuscles beginning to show through at the ends, my package might have been a man's thigh-piece, from groin to kneecap. Except for the odor, which gave us an unmistakable alibi. All the man at the Penn Station counter said was 'Uhn-uhn,' negative.

"My Bufano was a cheerful little rooster, he said we should try the Hotel Wentman, just a couple blocks over; they had a big checkroom, he said. No luck, they wouldn't take fish. We tried the Hotel Regina. No luck. We tried the Hampdon and the Marjoran. No and no. They wouldn't even let us all the way across the lobby at the St. Anselm. Mr. Bufano tried to rent a room at a little no-good place away over west, thinking we would put our salmon to bed in it, but they stopped us in the elevator.

"And so it was that at a few minutes before eight o'clock in the evening, we stood on a windswept corner in western Manhattan, and the tears welled up in my eyes and not even my pigeon, my Bufano, could comfort me. For suddenly I had realized that this parcel was more than a cut-off salmon. This was all my troubles, wrapped up in shabby newsprint. This was all the things that kept me from all my desires. That package—I suddenly realized it, Mrs. Manterbaum—that package was all the unhappinesses I couldn't get rid of in this life: it was my fleshiness, my unbeatable appetite for chocolate things, and my being without any learning, and no friends to speak of, and teased by such spiteful old maids as our Maggie, and couldn't even be promoted past the Near Pantry, and what good was I anyhow? And I was embracing all these things in my arms like a dear beloved friend, and smelling to high heaven of the burden.

"Then it was that my Bufano said, 'Well, Miss Peggety, three's a crowd, but let's face facts, he goes where we go.'

"And I suddenly realized you have to live with whatever it is you have to live with, so I dried up my eyes and said, 'Suits me, Mr. Bufano.'

" 'Well!' he beamed, and a gold tooth he had glistened like the planet Venus at the edge of night. 'What is it to be, steak or a little twinkletoes?'

"Now that I knew where I was, with my shortcomings folded up in a wee bundle of old papers, you might say, and my Bufano willing to accept them if I would, I grew bold suddenly and said, 'Couldn't we do both, Mr. Bufano? Eat and dance too?'

" 'Miss Peggety, you're a dear,' he said, and if I had cried this time, it would have been for other reasons than mere fishiness. My Bufano was so delicate!

"We had a grand time, I can tell you. My Bufano took me here and there, now dancing, now eating, now tippling a wee beer, now riding a Fifth Avenue bus just for the ride, as idle as you please. Soon we were used to our scaly friend and his consequences. What if everybody *did* turn and give us a stare, with tiny wrinkles at the bridge of the nose? In a way, it was gaudy, you might say. Surely Small Peggety had never in her life attracted so much attention, either from eye or nostril. I will go farther. Our salmon became more than a novelty: he was, at last, a handy thing to have about the person. In a crowded situation, we could always get passageway—the mob just opened up for us, real respectful. In the eating places (my Bufano took me to some of the basement ones, away to the fringes of the great city, where, either through kinship with the proprietor or a grand little tip, there was never a question of accepting us with our third party), we used it for a little extra table, beside us, to hold an ashtray or perhaps a wee pony of spirits. There it was, squared off at both ends, like a piece of log, and it stood up steady and true, very convenient by the knee for a reach. And there our hands did brush against one another: that was when I knew that my Bufano was the nicest one of all.

"Indeed, what except my parcel of shortcomings led to the bliss of the evening? I had to be back to the Near Pantry by seven in the morning, which meant, at the latest, the five-thirteen from Penn Station. It was still only about three in the morning when my Bufano, with the gentlest way in the world, said, 'My dear, don't you think that your salmon needs a little ventilation? I should hate, for your Mr. Saunders' sake, to have it fester and decay. It wants aeration. I propose that we go up to Central Park, and fold back the newspapers, and give it the night air to keep it tasty.'

"That we did. We found a wee hillock, away from the paved walks—'Asphalt!' my Bufano had remarked as we had gone along the walks. 'Your Mr. Saunders is everywhere'—and we set up our fish on the hill and peeled away the newsprint and let the sweet, damp night get at it. We moved away a little, to wait for the salmon to grow mellow, when, next thing I knew, as natural as the dew all around and the constellations winking up there, Bufano got his arms about me. He could just barely make it with his short little arms and my girth, which he praised. And he stood on tiptoe and kissed me."

Miss Peg's voice had fallen low; her eyelids shaded her jovial eyes in a modest downward look. Mrs. Manterbaum sighed.

"Did you catch your train?" Johnny the busboy asked.

"I caught my train, Johnny," Miss Peg said. "Yes, I caught my train." She paused. "I never saw my Bufano again, either. He was the hit-and-run sort, you might say. But I don't know, Johnny, it didn't matter. That night did something for me. You know, Mrs. Manterbaum, I have never been able to give sufficient worry to my faults since that night. Some would call me slack. . . . I don't know. . . . Yes, I caught the five-thirteen, Johnny."

"How was the fish next night?" Mrs. Manterbaum of the sweet tooth wanted to know.

"When they brought it out to the Near Pantry, after the second serving," Miss Peg replied, "I dared to cut away a wee snippet. I put it in my mouth. Oh heavens, Mrs. Manterbaum! It faded on the tongue. It put this angel cake of mine to shame. I rested the morsel against my palate and let it warm my throat, the way the men do with their brandy. And I'm not ashamed to tell you, Mrs. Manterbaum, that I said to myself, 'I'm not so bad as I thought, not half so bad.' . . . *Well!*" Miss Peg said abruptly and more briskly. "Time to lock up."

Miss Peg lifted the pan of delicacies and slid it onto the shelf where it belonged. She stood up and dusted the crumbs from the front of her dress, seeming to be rather pleased with herself.

Fling

"All you have to do is cross a river and you're in a foreign country?"

"That's right, Venus," Philip said.

"Let's really have one last fling. Let's go across the border. Let's go abroad."

Crossing that dirty little river to Ciudad Juárez would be, yes, a crossing. Ah, not quite a real one, not like the old days, going really abroad on the *Ile*—remember the food on the *Ile*?—sea bass *farçi* and those little paper-thin cucumber slices? That world of the heavenly ships was no more. Where had it gone? This crossing would be on foot, on a rickety bridge, in the dark of the night, and one would be trying to forget the pain. Never mind. "Let's do it tonight. I can't wait to tell Drua I've been abroad."

Every crossing, she'd once said, is an act of imagination. Walking unsteadily across that shabby bridge, tonight, to a dusty town in Mexico, one would have to try to imagine an ocean, a stateroom on the boat deck, portholes with the brass fittings shining like the hopes of all those years. She'd said that thing about crossing the ocean, she distinctly remembered, on the night of the party for Charley Trotter and Pam, their sixteenth wedding anniversary, at Cold Spring—God, how many years ago! That was also the night when that other thing happened, when nobody could persuade our Philip to rise to his feet to make the obligatory anniversary toast, and he began to rumble along seated—he was awfully tight but still he had that knack of his for the *mot juste*—and the rest of us—we were all so sozzled—scrambled out of our chairs and sat down on the floor, to establish the appropriate spacial relationship between orator and audience—the speaker pouring his words downward to his listeners—and down there we could see that Philip had his legs crossed and was kicking the upper one, showing off because during drinks Pam had suddenly gone over and curled up on his lap, and she'd reached up to her thigh and taken off that atrocious ruffled satin garter, with appliquéd hearts on it—she'd announced she could do without it because she had a garter belt on, too—and she'd given it to him, and now it was on his calf, over his trouser leg, kick kick kick as he droned on even though his audience had all disappeared under the table. On the terrace, after coffee and too many brandies, Sylvia threw Pam's slippers down the steep bank into the laurel, on account of the garter thing; Sylvia had a crush on our Philip even then, and she was jealous of Pam.

"Philip, darling," she said, "do you remember that thing of the garter?"

"You mean about Pam, that time? And Syllie? And Pam's shoes? Never forget it."

"God, how many years ago. It's all gone, darling."

How had the subject of crossings come up that night? Hard to remember. Some memories are so clear, some slip away like thieves. It was that night, though; that night when Sylvia was jealous of Pam over *my* Philip.

This trip of filthy Indians. Our Philip's romantic ideas were all very well when we were leaning against linen-covered pillows at 514, with a fireplace fire twinkling: Acoma! To see the rock of Acoma, where death came for the Archbishop! To see in one's mind Willa Cather, that imperious young sack of gravel and style, riding all those dusty, sun-stretched miles on horseback in a double-breasted suit and a Cavanaugh fedora with her female companion to see the church on the startling mesa with the timbers two feet thick and fifty feet long in the roof that had been hauled by Indians under the priests' whips from faraway Mount Taylor, what's *now* called Mount Taylor. Philip with those liquid warlock eyes could put you in an ecstatic trance, and the first thing you knew you were in a drawing room on the Super Chief having dinner brought when the Chablis was chilled enough, on your way to his vision of Acoma.

But the reality. When one learned that one had to walk up the col to the top of the mesa, to pay to see a lot of dirty Indian mud huts, it was easier, while Philip and the Pretz boy panted onward and upward, just to stretch out in the dust against the adobe wall beside that simply mountainous harpy of a souvenir-selling Indian granny, as big as Sampy Ferguson, who can't ride in taxis because the doors are too narrow. The old shamaness started out, waving her hands as if sprinkling dew over her junk on the cloth in the dust, with a couple of grunts of the sort she'd learned from movies that real live Indians use for conversing, but finally, when she saw I was just as tough as she, relaxed into some of the straightest talk you'll ever hear about her racket: going native. She had a black blanket over her shoulders, and she looked like Vivien, the Lady of the Lake, only she was fat and her lake was dust, sand and dust, bones and dust and sand.

But the trip had been all all all Indians, Mexicans, Negroes—swarms and swarms of the colored ones, various colors but a monotone of resentment of *us*. That's it, you see. It's all gone. We're the new minority. There was a time when a white Protestant person, with the backing of a letter of credit, was in charge of the whole tickety-boo, but now we're moving into a shadowy area; you hear them crowding and whispering, and the next thing you know they'll jostle you in the street and—unthinkable—spit. When you add the Jews, and the dark Irish—they've got that Moorish strain somewhere, and the sardonic lips. Oh, Philip, I tell you. "Darling, if I'm jostled by one more jig or spic or wetback or Big Chief Squattum-on-Ground! I've had it, my sweet."

"What talk, Venus. Hush, honey. We'll go abroad tonight and get a change of air."

"And get heartburn on those disgusting tamales."

"It'll be charming, Venus. They'll give us half a *limón* and some salt to suck off our wrist with the tequila."

"You're a fat shoat, just one interminable digestive system attached to a little suckling mouth."

"Oh, now, Venus, honey, it was your idea to go abroad."

"I know, but I'm tired of having all the ideas, Philip."

Here we are sitting in the bar of the Whatyoumaycallit Hotel, in El Paso, with a picture of Kennedy among the bottles, imagine having a new President who seems to be half your age—for we are seventy-nine, and he, our Philip, is a tagalong seventy-eight. But Philip is married to us, in sickness sickness and in health, and is steady behind the wheel of a Hertz Galaxie, that's the *big* Ford, he keeps saying, boring dear old stomach man, a dear, a dear. "You're a dear, my dear. Please pardon your poor little hag wife. Sometimes I don't think I can stand it."

"Venus."

"You're really very sweet to me, you know. Do we miss Sylvia?"

"Now, honey, please let's not have another quarrel."

"All that was aeons ago, in Prohibition actually. Who cares anymore?"

"You do."

"That's true, darling, I do. Passionately. That's why I'm so much younger than you are."

Why did we always travel around *à trois?* Sylvia that day on the white ship under the rainbow going into Gibraltar with a billion dolphins playing around the bow. A flutter of a Hermès scarf at her throat. The water all yellow at the edge of the tide change off the breakwater. Syllie was good for Philip for a year. The ennobling effect of love; you simply cannot do anything ignoble when you are near the loved one —except, perhaps, cheat on your dearest wife. How playful he was on that trip! He phoned up from the lobby of the Aletti in Algiers, when one was so worried, and one simply blurted, "Oh, you're *there*, Philip!"—relieved.

"No, I'm *here*," he said, "and you're *there*, Venus. You say I'm 'there'—'You're there, Philip'—but I'm here, and you're not here, so if you say I'm 'there,' and you're not 'there,' because you insist that 'there' is here, and 'here' is there, then where *are* you, Venus? . . . I say, are you there?"

I was worried even though Sylvia was not really interested in bed; she broke into a cold sweat when a man touched her, even by accident, so Philip felt like a lion, and I felt safe, though Philip was in fact cheating again, all over the place, but not with Sylvia, she was his protective coloration; he was cheating on both of us. Syllie had that quick cutting edge. She learned the entire Culbertson system really in twenty minutes; knew by ESP where every card was around the table. Her voice used to tremble when she started arguing with a weak man, and she always did—like a cat that can't help jumping into the lap of the only ailurophobe in the room.

"I have a headache."

"Thinking about Sylvia, Venus?"

"Damn you."

But you see, Philip is one of those rare people who are kind and good by nature, not one of those who become so after an extended inner struggle and may relapse. He has such odd dreams—of a motorcycle, just last night, in the shape of a tubelike red fire-enginey metal horse. The little Upmann cigar tube sticking out of his breast pocket. Dear Philip, a parlayer: he inherited money, married it, and made it, too. He exercises his money, as he does his kindly instincts, with a natural grace, for he's unostentatious and yet unerringly correct: he sensed the cummerbund was coming back the year before it did. He's sure of himself. I take partial credit for that. He knows he can count on his poor Venus. The night he gave me that nickname, before we'd ever even gone to bed together, we'd driven down after a party for a skinny-dip, and Pam, the bleeding heart, one charity committee after another, lost an earring, or said she did, in the sand, and squealed to Philip —they've *all* been after our Philip—to turn on the headlights, and by gorry she'd "lost" the earring right in their beam, and there she stood in her opulent Rubens altogether, bumping and grinding ever so subtly, her breasts like huge hot haggis puddings, but Philip, dear Philip, having no eyes for such a feast, met *me* as I came out of the water, with wet hair seaweed-runny on my face, to see what was going on, and he whispered, "You're so beautiful, my Venus on the half shell." Venus ever since.

I didn't know what he meant by the half shell until years later, when he marched me up those long stairs at the Uffizi and showed me the Botticelli.

One of the reasons, I suppose, that I'm so tired is that I haven't slept a wink—in bed, at least—on this whole trip; I doze and doze in the car, the red rocks a blur along the edges of the cinemascope, nodding through a budget Western. This really is the Sandman's Land, but at night he doesn't sprinkle my eyes, he grits my teeth. At Canyon de Chelly—which our traveling companion, the Pretzel, had told us was such a "dolling little crack in the earth's crust," he can't say "darling"—they petrified you by setting out in a jeep with grotesque balloon wheels because, as they loudly announced, there was danger of quicksand in the foot of the canyon, gobbling up ordinary cars, a party of four from Minnesota had been swallowed just last Tuesday, nothing left but a visored straw cap. On the walls of the caves, above the primitive dwellings and the ancient pictographs, you saw the archaeologists' signatures—was it Schliemann who dug up Troy signing the cavern wall like Kilroy Was Here? But the point was this generator, poppety poppety all the living night, across the way from us, and bourbon wouldn't stop it, pounding wouldn't stop it, weeping wouldn't stop it; and even an offer of money by our Philip at two o'clock in the morning would neither stop it nor get us another bungalow. And little Pretz slinking around murmuring about the dolling canyon.

Money wouldn't stop it. There are some things you just know in advance money won't stop, but there's no real harm in trying, our Philip says. Because, you see, we looked at the world and made a basic decision: spend it. Dump it at any cost. It's poison, both to have and not to have. But if you don't have it at least you have an incentive to get it—something to live for. . . . Oh, come now, one has really lived for moments like that one on the terrace at Agrigento, hasn't one, Venus? Hasn't one? When we first walked out on that shiny *terrazzo Veneziano* surface and almost swooned at that evening's first look at the Sicilian hills and the enchanted sea? Wasn't there a time when a mere *view* was enough to live for?

But think what has happened to the charming golden nymphs and fauns who were at that party for Charley and Pam. Syllie—a full vial of sleeping pills. Charley—a regular one in Reno, a quickie in Mexico, another full-term one in Reno, another quickie in Alabama, and constantly jobless, not that he ever needed a job: a rolling stone gathers no boss. And

Pam, fighting for her causes and sleeping around up the ladder, until, poor ambitious girl, she married that battling liberal with the spongy nose, Senator Tadpole, or whatever his name is, who promptly got unseated the next November. Pam, Pam, you luscious Puritan! And Sue-Sue in and out of Riggs; and Frickie on the booze; and weren't the Jellinans there?

"Darling, what ever happened to Hugo Jellinan?"

"He disappeared."

"What do you mean, 'disappeared'?"

"He dribbled all his money down some mine shaft in Chile. He just stopped being around. Someone told me they saw him in, he was living in, Quincy, Illinois, I think, some unbelievable hole like that."

You see? Our Philip is the only survivor. He hasn't changed one bit. Stormy strong man. Oh, darling, what I'd give to have one or two of these middling decades to do over again with you! Mephisto, come bargain with me. I'll give you some delightful considerations. I wouldn't want the very youngest decades; something riper.

"What would you think of being forty again?"

"Well"—what a responsive one he is!—"first we'd take that sailing trip down the Windward Islands, and at Tobago Cay we'd moor right against the sandbank in the gut there, and after dinner the crewboys would play for us—that out-of-tune guitar and the tiny flute-fife making a yellowbird's song high in a banyan tree—and they'd sing; 'Mary Ann': I love that line, '*All day long she's sifting sand,*' I see her on a beach with little children crowding around her, she's some kind of sex saint. . . . '*All day long—*' "

"Don't sing, darling. You spoil the effect."

Our eyes are closed. We are riding down the trade winds on a broad reach under the lee skirts of Martinique: the high cone of the Grand Piton with a cloud for a hat. A call for elevenses, rum and lime. A smelly cheese and some Huntley & Palmer water crackers. Blue sea like a lifetime ahead.

"Remember Ubo?" Philip says. Mulatto child we were told about, given name actually U-Boat, born the proper number of months after a Nazi submarine surfaced in Marigot Bay and a foraging party went ashore for fish and vegetables.

"Don't keep talking about what the whites have done to the coloreds, Philip. It makes me jumpy. I *told* you I have a headache."

"How about a pause that refreshes?"

"What time is it?"

"Two-forty."

"We really ought to have some lunch. Bother, I've lost interest in lunch. Tell that dear man to build me a Grand-Dad highball, Philip."

Philip, who cannot get the bartender's eye, though we are the only ones in the bar, is too well-bred to snap his fingers or hiss or clap—there's a sort of permanent Links Club hush about Philip—gets up and goes over. We can see from our seat that this El Paso mestizo barman doesn't have the time of day for the highball bit, a fleeting moment of disgust, a shadow of buzzard's wings crossing over his face. He pulls at the ears of his dirty monkey jacket. A glare on the glazed wall is reflected from a passing car in the street. There's a circular mirror, with a border of wreathed leaves, and a portrait of our new President, Jack Kennedy, sitting on a glass shelf at the center of the mirror, grinning at us. Captive ambers of booze are lit from behind by a fluorescent light which flickers, sending coded messages to the moths of the world. Two or three moths flap *in extremis* among the bottle necks. We are overcome with sadness; we begin to weep.

"Venus! Venus pie!" Philip, coming back, flipping at the sight of tears, says in his baby-talk voice that is so incongruous coming from the end who caught Hobey Clark's pass in the last quarter of the Harvard game in senior year and carried the ball—he says to this day it felt as heavy as a mail sack full of stock certificates, a crazy image, because he wasn't a runner on the Street until the next year—seventy-three yards to score. He wants to know what's got us sloppy.

"It's the whole thing, Philip. Whatever do you suppose possessed Syllie?" To take enough pills to reach the longer sleep. Long ago.

"You and your headache," Philip says, and there's a bead on the edge of his voice; he hones it off with a single stone blasphemy. "Christ."

At once the weight in my chest levitates, and I feel fine. "Did runners have to go in the mail room back when you first went to work for Peters, Silliman? I mean, they wouldn't have those snippety little executive trainees doing anything sordid like that now, would they?"

"We didn't have a mail room. It was all one big bullpen."

"Why do you blow a gasket every time I mention Syllie?"

"Why do *I*? Darling, I think you got sunstroke yesterday when we stopped for that picnic."

Our bottom hurts. We ask Philip to be an angel and go up to the room and get us our lifesaver, as we call it, a little tubular rubber ring our bottom-doctor prescribed for us that has a petit-point slipcover we made last summer with a motif of vine leaves. I think it's darling; Pam tells me she thinks the petit point calls attention to "it," as she calls my pain, but I ask her, Wouldn't the bare rubber call attention to it more? I mean, carrying the object around, entering a room. You see, I think many people do things in the name of honesty that are really not quite straight. Certainly "honesty," the way Syllie used to bandy it about, can become at times the moral equivalent of assault and battery. I don't think it hurts to cover hurts—the bandage principle of human intercourse —maybe I'm Victorian but I can't help it. Syllie couldn't help it either. She didn't mean to be cruel; she said she was honest.

While Philip is gone I wink at the bartender and he brings me a refill. He is charming. The Spanish *s*. "Escuse me, Miss.

You 'ave esscotch?" Imagine the inborn courtesy, calling a
ruined fortress like me "Miss." No, that was my husband who
had the Scotch, mine was bourbon. He gets the drink and
chats with me; he has had a couple himself; don't forget it,
bartenders tell their own troubles just as much as they listen
to others'. He is delightful. A sort of lugubrious pinchy behavior simply because I am a woman. I was beautiful once;
Philip made me believe that. Venus. This Manuel sees it in
me. When you deal with the coloreds individually, you can
get along swimmingly, each one can be a joy. It's the mass,
the abstract, that's so hard to think about. Of course this
Manuel is only partly colored. He is talking about the Kansas
City Athletics, for some reason, and I try to imagine what it
would be like if we, the white Protestants, were the bartenders
and mop women everywhere, and the coloreds were the tip
givers. Of course our Philip would be splendid. Basically he
likes people, and I really don't think it comes from being rich;
he received good tough fiber in his chromosomes. He would
make a topnotch railway porter, for instance, truly first-rate.
Oh, I can see him cheerfully flipping up the drawing-room
berth along about Elizabeth, New Jersey, on the way in, with
a jolly loud *clankety-clank* to waken the grumpy ace of spades
in the lower in the next compartment who shouted in such an
ugly way at Philip's colleague, the white Protestant room-
service waiter from the dining car, the night before. It certainly
is a changing world we live in.

Philip is back. He notices I have forged ahead on my own;
not a flicker of disapproval. Philip's magnanimity has kept me
from drinking too much. Sue-Sue was always frowning and
shaking her head at Frickie, and look at him, you can't call
him a lush; lush is too soft. He's a roaring souse. I can't take
him anymore.

When you thought about it, all of life had been one last
fling. I mean, when you live with a man who lets live, it all
has a rampant feeling, headlong, estral, tropical.

"Was I beautiful?"

"You had a wart on the end of your nose, and your left titty sagged."

"Beast."

But the teasing joke has left Philip grave. "Darling, you're thin. We really should have lunch."

"I'm not so bad. I weighed myself yesterday. A hundred and three pounds with nothing on but my shoes and bracelets." I never was big.

"Oh, yes"—it was easy to *say* it, leaning against the pillows at 514, on a foggy December evening, when you knew that the cheery lights on the Christmas trees along the archipelago of New York Central islands on Park Avenue were going to bounce off your bedroom ceiling and keep you awake until real light came, and then you'd sleep on a tide rip of dreams; it was easy to *say* it—"we'll have one last fling, Philip. We'll see your writer friend in our imaginations, riding a horse to Acoma."

But doing the thing was not so easy. Lifesaver or no lifesaver.

The moment one stood on the platform in Albuquerque, and the heat waves came whispering around like a flock of Mediterranean beggars that won't go away, you knew it was not going to be easy. But you knew you had to make a show of ease, for Philip's sake. The price one pays for having a kind man at one's elbow.

Philip drove us in his drive-it-himself, the *big* Ford, out of Albuquerque's small-townish main drag, with Pretz huddled in the back seat getting over the trots—"My heinie hoits," he said in his city tongue, not aware of my problem—as we skimmed over dead terrain to Laguna. There were signs all along the road inviting you to come in and inspect live snakes. A stillness on the hills, as if all that glare were some kind of midnight on fire. I saw sand dunes lapping over one crest, and on one dusty razorback rise it looked as if a thin cloud were passing over, though the sky was an empty brass scuttle. Far off there were forests on the mountains.

Gradually we moved into an earlier era, a time of mesas and buttes, and in a wink Philip, stopping the big Ford and checking his AAA triptik—one thing I loathe about our Philip is that he always plans ahead—suddenly turned off Route 66 onto a dirt road. All those frightful TV Westerns: hills of rock where the bad guys know the footholds—tan and brown, no reds. The Enchanted Mesa, standing alone in its trance; rounded shoulders, wrinkles and faults. Holes on the faces: gun emplacements? God, God, whom do we have to fight now?

And then, before we had a chance even to imagine Willa in her double-breasted suit on a skinny packhorse, her eyes burning with a fever of perfect sentences, there it was. Acoma. A big dirty round rock with a dirty village perched up as high as it could get, like Enna or Troina or any of those hilltop Sicilian villages: you'd be led to guess that humanity was a woman who'd seen a mouse.

I was thinking: Dearest Philip, I have so much pain. I am going to die. Except that I cannot bear to leave you, my close friend Philip. I'll stay as long as I can, dear heart. I was thinking rather dramatic thoughts as he parked the Galaxie at the foot of the staggering cliffs whose rounded shoulders seemed to have been eroded, the way sea-washed boulders are, by the sun's everlasting rays crashing down on the rocks like breakers.

Parking? Do you mean we're supposed to *walk* up? Ha! Thank you, not for the entire first printing of *Death Comes for the Archbishop*. Death came to a good place to find the old boy, I'll say that, if this was where He found him. I slumped on the stone steps of the cabin at the foot, and I said to the big

Indian woman selling pottery souvenirs there, "*¿Cóm' estás?*"
I knew it was the wrong language, I was teasing.

She grunted. "Ugh." This was to keep prices up on her
junk.

Afterward we had a picnic in a grove of cottonwoods beside
the dirt road on the way back out to 66. Pretzel said in his
fluty Manhattan dialect, "I catch why they call 'em cottonwoods." He was picking up bits of lint off the forest floor like
a cleaning woman. Philip opened a bottle of Almadén and,
gnashing away at the sandwiches we'd had made up in Albuquerque, he told me about the rock of Acoma, where Death
came.

He and the Pretz had started up a sandy trail when an Indian
woman had shrieked down from the cliff, "Go up the
stairway!"—pointing. Twisting up through crevices, stone
steps cut away, steep places with handholds. Telling this,
Philip was in high spirits, chewing and regaling his Venus.
By God, I love you, you difficult lusty man. The Indian woman
was waiting for them at the top in a checked shirt and blue
jeans, looking like a Jap high-school girl.

"What's dat boid?" Pretz said, pointing to a bedraggled,
half-molted brownish bird.

"Robin bird," the Indian woman said. Guides all over the
world tell lies. But the Pretzel lived in a city tower and didn't
know the difference.

They registered and went around and saw everything: the
great mud church for the glory of God with the primitive
painting at the altar of St. Stephen, which, seen as magic,
had been stolen by another tribe and the Acomans, or Aco-
mites, or whatever they are, had had to go all the way up to
the Supreme Court to get it back; the little Jap high-school
girl posing as an Indian babbled her lies among the dirty
houses with mica windows like sealed portholes. Where was
Death? You see, Philip with his vitality simply pushed Him

over the cliff, the way the Indians in the double-breasted-suit woman's story carried Friar Balthazar from his airy loggia with its peach tree and threw him from the edge into eternity.

My pain ebbed away as I listened to Philip.

They went back in the registration house for shade. A man was there trying to give three boxes of apples to the registration woman. He was a white Protestant who for purest of reasons felt sorry for poverty-ridden pigmented natives, but he was angry at being taken for just another tourist. He had been there before. Didn't she remember him? He was shaking, perhaps from the climb with the apples, perhaps from the cold bath of ingratitude he was taking. The woman curtly said it would be easiest to descend by the sand trail. He said he preferred the stone stairs; he'd been there before. Straining for control, he asked the woman if she knew how to fry apples, these were frying apples. They should be consumed in a certain definite order of containers. Some had worms. And you saw that he had kept the best apples at home.

The bartender swishes a horse-tail whisk after the flies, greedy little beer lovers. I feel a flicker of anger.

"Couldn't we have let it go at that, when we'd seen Acoma?" After all, the idea had been to see that rock; the trip was to be a species of casual allusion, and that was all. We like this about our Philip: he's an intelligent man, educated, one guesses, *despite* St. Paul's and Yale, the school with little wooden cubicles and the college with the great mute tomb of Scroll and Key—big men went Bones, the right men went Keys, they said, the ones who wore tails so often that they developed a bit of billiard-table green in the serge of the suit. Those were white-tie days, and here was one possible definition of the best of breeding: a slightly moldy look to your tails. But our Philip liked books even then, and always had, convention be damned. As with the cummerbund, he was a jump ahead of the pack—Henry James under his belt in 1935, long before the surge of fashion; Kafka and, yes, Kierkegaard by 1945. He used to talk to me about each book. Now Willa Cather was only a fortnight's going to sleep with a novel; he wasn't mad for the story but he said he sort of liked her scrollwork. Acoma, a December thought over martinis.

But no, once there we had to go on. And on. Canyon de Chelly. An overdrifted road, like a Robert Frost snapshot of melancholy, except for burning silicates in place of snow, to Dinnehotso, Kayenta, Monument Valley: Dior hats in stone. The Grand Canyon; I mean, *really!* Oak Creek Canyon, a sudden dampness, ivy growing so fast down the bedstead post you could almost hear it tick. Tuzigoot. Montezuma Castle. Endless, endless.

And now this incredible barren barroom, with the round mirror with a wreath engraved on it such as Great Caesar sported, and our baby-boy President smiling at us from his shelf.

"I'm tired, Philip. Let me go home to New York." I want to die in my own bed.

"Darling. You'd never have been able to justify coming all the way to the Southwest for Acoma alone."

"Everything comes out of a storybook with you."

"I mean, it would have been uneconomical, honey."

A peal of laughter. It is from my own throat. "You're a funny man, my dear. You're so quick about some things. You know, I never have been able to conceive how with all your brains you could sit there night after night at the Links in that atmosphere like the inside of an old velvet-lined violin case with such truly truly stupid men as Skilly Waters and Danforth Cochran. All right, you tell me they're Chairmen of Boards, and Skilly's a wizard helmsman, very shrewd about wind shifts on the Sound. And then I have to ask: Darling, how do those businesses survive? I mean, Skilly is *dumb*. What do you *say* with him?"

"I say, 'Five diamonds.' And he says, 'Pass.' "

"Brilliant."

I worry about the future of American business. Skilly came for dinner once, and in the corner of the sunburned cockleshells of one of his ears he overheard our Philip say something about Henry Esmond; he'd taken up Thackeray. "Esmond," Skilly said, barging in. "Belong to the Beach Club? He the one just bought Chub's Atlantic? Stupid buy that boat. All pulled up at the bow. Not enough waterline. What you say fellow's name that bought it?"

Philip wants to appease me. "Skilly has clever little people working for him."

"Thank heavens. But why are all people who are clever, or industrious, always 'little'?"

Philip doesn't answer that. He sees that we're getting that old two-drink belligerence, comes on when you hardly hope for it, like a second wind. After that, third-drink thaw, an access of tenderness. After that—ah, well, by then it may be time to have a bath and a pretend nap before going abroad.

It's odd; for our Philip, the Links was a matter of course, he was asked to join and he did. But Skilly, who'd lasted two years, anyway, at Groton, and was much richer than Philip, and taller, and going right to the top in a business that didn't even belong to his family—Skilly was frantic about getting in. Came to Philip and asked him to rally round some solid seconders. Kept telephoning: when would it be decided?

When did I first think about dying? Long before Sylvia died by her own delicate hand with the ruby on it I always envied, a sweet sparkling drop of life on the cold bitch hand that would steal her away from us. Her hands and feet were always blocks of ice, and her nates. "Chilly ahss," our Philip would say. Syllie's shiver!

"Do you think you could get the bartender to turn the air-conditioning down? It's like the North Pole in here."

Philip goes over and tries; the bartender says the room isn't air-conditioned. Philip looks at me closely as he sits again. Risking my little spurting tantrums, he says, as if to swoop me up and carry me off on his white steed, rescuing me from whatever austral wind has breathed on me, "Remember the night you thought the Age of Electricity had come to an end?"

That was in my drinking period—God, how many years ago—and I was very drunk. A party at the Trotters', I remember I'd just been dancing in the bay window with Charley, and I said, "Charley, you're the *hardest* man," and he pulled a big silver cigarette case out of his breast pocket to show me what the hardness was, when one of those sudden August line squalls came through; there was a sizzling thrill of lightning and a flat loud crack on its shirttails, and the lights went out, and I began to sob because I thought the Age of Electricity had ended forever. We were going to have to go back to pumping water by hand with long-handled pumps, and there'd be a faint odor of alcohol when you read a book by one of those bright lamps with gauze mantles which vanished at a touch when they were cool. I cried and cried.

"You're just trying to remind me that I was a drunken slob."

"Venus, you were charming. So worried about how I'd have to crank my car—wasn't that the Diana?—to get home because the starter wouldn't work, and when I said the spark plugs wouldn't work either, you said you'd never liked the Diana anyhow."

"You bought the Diana because I was Venus. It was very ugly of you."

"You doted on it."

"Don't you scold me about cars. Those Jag seats."

Philip used to have a different car every year. Pierce-Arrow.

Packard. Cadillac. Imperial. Continental. And earlier: a Cord, the Diana, a Maxwell, a Franklin, even a Jordan Playboy. Some years an affectation like a Chevrolet. Never intimidated by the fact that the Proper Thing was to stick to one not-too-gaudy make—say, Olds, the big Olds. Always claimed that each car he owned was the best-engineered bus in American industrial history. Then he bought a black Chrysler convertible and wanted some red leather seats installed in it that he'd seen on a Jag. The dealer said that would be out-of-sight expensive. "Tell you what," our splendid Philip said. "Let me know when a hopelessly wrecked Jag comes in." He'd pick up some seats for a song. He only had to wait three days.

I ask, "Where's your odious Pretzel?"

"I don't know. Out buying buildings, I guess."

Julius Shonekind Pretz came along for the ride. He's one of the New Type. It used to be that white Protestants had almost all the money that counted; I mean, you didn't count suits or shoes or slot machines; I mean oil, minerals, railroads. Fifth Avenue, along the Park. Collections of Impressionists. But now. There's this New Type. It hasn't gone to Hotchkiss. It hasn't a prayer of getting into the Beach Club. It talks decidedly funny. But listen, it's very bright, very amusing, very warmhearted, and so rich it makes you dizzy to think about it. A wonderful earthy quality that no one I've ever known ever had. Into everything. Mike Wallace interviews him, would Mike Wallace ever interview Skilly Waters? I make fun of the Pretzel's accent; it isn't that bad. He doesn't say "boid," he says something that's ironically just off the edge of the fake-English-accent "böd" you used to hear the Brearley girls saying. Where did the money come from? Not entirely clear. The only thing that's crystal is that it didn't come from his daddy. He can talk about anything: breeder reactors, the other day. "Sounds like sending old atom bombs out to stud," our Philip said. The trouble is, here we are *à trois* again. I want to be alone with Philip for this last fling, and that's why I call the Pretzel odious at the moment.

It's all very well to joke about death, atomic bombs, but your jokes on that Topic have to have a certain innocence, as I think Philip's do. Or Meredith's. My poor son Meredith. That innocent thing he said, accepting death as a casual occurrence, God how many years ago, when our Philip took him, much too young, really, seven or eight, to the Bowl, evidently expecting to make a man of his son by exposing him early to the manly game. Masses of Yale players were hurt during the game, "shaken up" they say on television, that box of mendacity, but this was back long before TV when the Blue played places like Vanderbilt and Georgia, and the Yalies were carried off the field on stretchers in flocks. On the way out of the Y-Men's special parking lot by Coxe Cage, we came to that big cemetery on the other side of Derby Avenue, and Meredith, after holding his breath till we were past, said, "Daddy, is that where they bury the Yale players?" He was serious: that's the true innocence of discussing that certain Topic.

But this trip in the desert: even if we'd left the Pretzel home, we'd have been *à trois* in the desert. The Topic rides along. Perhaps it's only what Pam calls "it" that makes me obsessed with this idea. I wish I were in my own bed.

For instance. Window Rock the other day. The rock window: the red of the rock makes a sharp jumpity edge against the blue of the sky. My pain is coming on. Our very whispers echo against the great concave pan of the red rock. We drive out through the picnic ground and around the Reservation headquarters. Along a newly surfaced tar road through a beautiful forest of ponderosa pine on the way to Ganado. We stop and eat lunch under a gnarled juniper, and I refuse to crack my hard-boiled egg on my head, as Philip does his, saying my own shell is too fine, finer probably than an egg's, but the truth is I'm afraid a bang on my noggin will knock all my guts out of my desperate bottom, which is now raging, raging.

I am very brave. We have a bottle of rosé, and there is a cool breeze. I make Philip burn the trash; the day before, I insisted on taking it along, and we left it in the motel room. I don't believe in strewing the wild places with our offal. Then, off the Ganado road, as I think I must die, must die, must die, we come to St. Michael's Mission, where the perpendicular sun is the Topic's emissary in the dusty courtyard. A Franciscan monk walks bareheaded across the yard in his brown habit and up onto the porch of the big building and puts a nickel in the slot of a Coke machine and takes a frosted bottle out. My pain ebbs away, and I give thanks to the God of that place, to whom I am, I guess, a stranger, for I have always been a heathen, but sometimes I thank God, so great is His bounty, whoever He is. Is He a Jew? A Jesuit? Does He have the Coke concession? Then why did the monk use a nickel?

"Do you think Meredith is happy?"

"Happy? Happy? What is 'happy'? Honey, you're so old-fashioned."

I've always wished he wouldn't call me "honey," it's tacky, déclassé, none of our kind uses that word. Philip doesn't care about certain lines of propriety, he cares terribly about others. But I must answer that urgent question of his. What is "happy"? I don't know whether I can say it right, but "happy" is something you and I, Philip, have occasionally been when we were playing gin rummy, perhaps, I don't know—when we've had that feeling of sneaking into each other's secrets. " 'Happy,' " I say flatly, "is a game of gin rummy. See if the bartender has some cards."

The bartender has no more cards than he has air-conditioning. "Manuel!" I call across the bar as Philip comes back. "*Su leche.*" The nice man in a dirty monkey jacket—I almost said to myself the nice little man—can't believe his ears. He shrugs his shoulders. I suddenly hope, hopelessly, that he hasn't heard me.

The reason the Topic throws me into such anger is that life

has been so good to me. There's a certain kind of hairy velvety weed on Long Island, with light green leaves and a big phallic something or other it erects in August, monstrous, whew; I sat down in a meadow and studied one of those, one summer—oh, it was *after* my drinking period but still a long time ago, God! But the point is, when you looked at it closely, it was so intricate, so cleverly done, really just as astonishing in its way as my expensive *Shiro-fugen* cherry tree when it gets all dressed up in its pink housecoat in the spring. A lousy weed. Manuel! I love you. I didn't mean that. I don't know what I'm saying when I swear in a foreign language.

"No, darling, what I mean about Meredith, he's a Good Soldier, he had a fine career in the war, all those ribbons, and there weren't many of his classmates who made chicken colonel, I *hate* that expression, but Philip, why did he *stay* in the Army? That was such a cautious outcome, such a *mild* thing to do. He's so mild, Philip. You're a slam-bang man, and I'm pretty keen on life, too, even if I have that tentative thing you're always talking about, but what happened with our boy? What do you think happened?"

"Drua happened."

Drua is now my maid. No one can pack a better bag, but I'm so blind without my glasses that I can't see what she's put in. I've been wearing this black sweater and these black slacks this whole trip; I don't dare dig in because I can never find my glasses the first thing in the morning. Philip finds them for me. For years Drua was Meredith's nurserynanny. I think Philip means not Drua affirmatively but that I neglected my son. Would that make him mild?

"Drua is a living angel. Don't you try again to talk me into firing her. What have you got against her? Is she blackmailing you? Did you tweak her behind the pantry door?"

Drua is one of the coloreds, and she is also one of the few Good Guys that are left. No bitterness in her. Except lately she's been having opinions about elections, she wouldn't have dreamed of having opinions in the old days. You see. It's beginning. They're whispering. They've even gotten to my Drua, who adores me.

Somebody on some ship on some crossing quoted Horace to us—why does this come to me now?—Drua packing me off?—to the effect that "he who hurries across a sea changes only the sky, not his own mind." I am afraid of this little river we are going to cross tonight. Oh, yes, and I remember now who said it, the great pianist, maestro of the ego, Anton Antonin, white lion's mane and tipping forehead and knobby hammer hands with fingers like Jerusalem-artichoke roots. Maiden voyage of the *Lizzy*. Outwardly cynical, but what did he play best? Chopin ballades. He had a Grand Marnier soufflé for a heart and an athlete's frame: fiercely sentimental. He spoke nine languages but hated "foreigners"—meaning anyone wherever he was—and was full of warnings about going abroad. I was young, and he took me on the deck tennis court between dances, it was my everybody-lies-down-with-every-body phase. One night in the salon he spoke of an Indian sage—was it Sardi?—who warned, "If you travel abroad, oh brother, carry your own stones, for there are dogs in every town. Do not suffer the anguish of the traveler who, arriving at a village, was greeted by barking dogs, and he reached down for a stone and discovered one, but to his dismay he found it fastened to a rock by a chain, and he cursed a village where fierce dogs run free and stones are chained." I remember this warning more vividly than my unfaithfulness to Philip on the deck tennis court. I was unfaithful often.

And now I am unarmed with stones. I hear barking.

Philip is after me about our son, and I feel that I *must* think about Meredith.

"It's normal for people Meredith's age to be mild," Philip is saying. "All of the middle generation now are mild. We older people are eccentrics, we are real, and the young ones have this Beat thing they don't know what to do with—they're unreal. But the in-between ones—they're bland, Venus, they're skimmed milk. Why do you worry so about Merri?"

"When I said 'mild,' I didn't mean colorless, I meant unfeeling."

"Don't you think that might be control? Maybe there's too much feeling rattling around inside there."

It's perfectly true that I didn't know anything about being a mother. When Meredith was small he had a cloth bear with a painted clowny face, and it got too ratty for words, and I sent it to the cleaners, and it came back blank, so I got Tilman Furness, he did those smashingly clever illustrations for children's books, he was a bit of a flit but he was the absolute tops in his line, to paint a new face on it, and what he did was so original, so sophisticated, as if a bear could be a sort of lech, raffish and sexy, and when I presented it to Meredith he screamed for three hours and promptly got croup that night. I was furious with him. After all, you didn't get Tilman Furness for peanuts.

Why shouldn't I have left most things to Drua? She was— she is—the salt of the earth. Meredith would lie with his cheek on that bosom of hers, an expanse of June, a bank whereon a wild thyme blew, and I just knew he was blissful, and it terrified me. Once on her day off I tried putting on her uniform, to see if he'd put his cheek where he could hear the pounding of my anxious heart, but it was bags too big for me, and anyway Meredith was always able to see through deceptions, even at two years old. He laughed as hard as if I were a Punch-and-Judy show.

"The mildness of the in-betweens," Philip says, "comes from their hopelessness, I guess. They see that money isn't it, after all. Whereas the young ones, the Beats and the off-Beats—"

"The whoozis?"

"As off-Broadway is to Broadway. Not the real thing but more interesting. I mean the talented upper-upper ones, good colleges. They just can't believe everything is hopeless, and still they don't know what to hope for."

"And what, pray, does that have to do with poor Meredith?"

"I was thinking of Chum. I know you don't like thinking about being a grandmama, Venus."

Charles, called Chum, the youngest of Meredith and Sally's three, got into Yale on the basis of the legacy, everyone says. His principal extracurricular activity is getting filthy. Fingernails like auto drippings on the garage floor. Never any shoes or socks, his big smelly feet propped up on Sally's cloisonné cigarette box on the coffee table, reciting Rimbaud and Baudelaire by the measured mile. But Chum smiles at me over his lurid toenails. I'm onto him. His trouble is simple. He's too much older than his years. Young people start everything so early now that they're not nearly so young as parents treat them, as Meredith treats *him*. After all, African girls—I'm onto the coloreds again, they're like ads, you can't dodge them—get married when they're twelve, thirteen. Our young ones could do that. Know what Chum wants? He wants a job: oh, he doesn't want to be an enforced patriot sent to the Cameroons on a bloody lying Truth Mission in place of military duty; no, he wants to be given credit for being what he really is, a middle-aged square masquerading as a nineteen-year-old off-Beat, as our Philip calls him. Chum grins at me over his cruddy tootsies because he knows I know.

My complaint about Meredith is that he pussyfoots right down the middle. He's neither Democrat nor Republican. Look at the ones he's voted for—each time, as he said, "with misgivings": Roosevelt over Landon, Willkie over Roosevelt, Dewey over Truman, Stevenson over Ike, Ike over Stevenson, and this last time Jack over who was that loathsome character? Cautious and doubtful every time. I like some violent zigzag in a man, I like extremes. Passion. The want of caution that results in discoveries, assignations, vivid Toulouse-Lautrec stuff, bouts of disgusting temper, sprees, big trombone passages, too much Peking duck, bankruptcy, divorce—don't you *dare*, Philip—juicy headlines of all sorts. I like a *man*. Meredith reads the *Times* and *Trib*; Philip reads the *News* and *Journal-American*. You should see Philip reading the paper: he reacts like a tyke in the Fun House, bounces, cackles, roars with anger at Booby Sokolsky's column, reads out loud: "Listen to *this*: 'GIRL ELEVEN HAS BABY IN CLASSROOM—*Little School-mates Assist in Delivery.*' " He's so rough and ready. And yet he's so so tender with me; my Nurserynanny Philip.

"I just wish Meredith wouldn't put on his rubbers every time a cloud appears."

"Drua taught him that. Her wetness madness. Drua grew up on the edge of a cypress swamp. Bayou or something."

"Wet didies. Do you think that pursy look around his mouth comes from toilet training? Maybe I *can* blame Drua. Wouldn't that be nice?" I am now able to dismiss the subject.

It is getting dimmer in the bar, perhaps the sun has gone behind a building. Manuel is rattling and banging. Lemon squeezer, heavy soda-split cap remover, that nice spiral wiry thing that keeps the ice in the shaker when he's pouring out marts, *whankety-whank*—he's washing his implements, throwing them down. He has the Latin temper. He's furious about what I said.

"Manuel!" I call.

"Essame all aroun'?"

"No. *Ven acá, amigo.* I want to talk to you."

He looks doubtful but comes over.

"Listen, sweetie," I say, "you mustn't let an old old bad-tempered woman throw you." I want to say, How breathtaking you are, you beautiful intricate hairy weed.

"Un Granddath, un esscotch," he says, and turns away.

Philip puts his hand on mine. Philip always understands.

I was unfaithful often, and yet the thought of Sylvia, the one
woman I'm fairly sure Philip *didn't* cheat on me with, in the
flesh anyway, still throws me into a loop-de-loop. The way
they used to *whisper* to each other. On that Sewanahaka
schooner, Frick Miller's boat. There were five of us that
time—*à cinq*, that's where you get really complicated, there's
always a floater, so to speak. Frickie, Sue-Sue, Philip, Syllie,
and Venus Surprised. We'd come along the Elizabeth Islands
from Quisset. It had been so quiet in that snug little bay
overnight except for Frick and Susan bickering; the bickers
flew ashore from us like flocks of gulls. Anyway, the idea was
to picnic and swim in Quicks's Hole and then go around to
Tarpaulin Cove for the night. I think the basic trouble was
that Frick was making a halfhearted play for me; he didn't
mean anything personal, it was just a habit. Frickie was handsome in a pretty-boy way—dark hair that was perfect for
cruising, it got sort of packaged in the wind, over a noble
shrine of a forehead, peeky eyes, and a spoiled mouth. I forget
his nose. There were no stinkpots in Quicks's for once, and
of course we swam in our skin-and-bones; we'd done this so
much we knew each other's bodies all too well—the big mole
on Sue-Sue's rib cage, Frickie uncircumsised and rather
astonishing—so that on the rare occasions when for some
reason modesty was enforced, it was rippingly sexy to see each
other in bathing suits. Really sort of aphrodisiac. Clothes make
sense. The human body is a bumpy, pale, hair-blotched affair
under an August sun on a scimitar beach a few miles off Cape
Cod. But oh, it was good to be young. Frick put up the
awning. We had rum, the drink that's so melty in the sun
that you always brought the limit home from the West Indies,
or especially from Cuba when you still could go to Varadero,
and then you could never bear to touch it in New York; rum
and March slush don't mix. Sue-Sue made sandwiches, popping

an ugly swift little gull out of her mouth every few seconds. After lunch, Sylvia—she was wearing, with her usual just-opened effect, a Basque thing and a big incongruous floppy garden-party straw hat because her skin was made of rolled-out candles—said to our Philip, "Darling, let's go forward and take a nap." It turned out she meant not the foredeck but the fore cabin. They disappeared down the forward hatch. I knew nothing could happen with her, but after half an hour, with Frick nuzzling me in a yawny way, I thought I'd scream with fear for my beloved Philip, so I pretended I had to go to the head, and there they were, lying crown to crown in the separate pipe bunks which made a V in the slice-of-pie crew's cabin, just abaft the chain locker, whispering. Not touching, except for the fingertips of their maddening secrets. I went in the head and threw up, my cheeks crimson in the knowledge that that susurrating pair, veed together out there, could hear my retches. Then that damnable crapper pump, with its in-valves and out-valves; I was in there half an hour sweating tanks and tanks, and they were out there softly whispering—about *what*?

"Darling, what did you and Sylvia use to whisper about?"

"Don't think about Sylvia, Venus. Please. It gives you a headache."

"I already *have* a headache."

"About perfect you. We whispered about how perfect you were."

"You make me sick to my stomach."

"No, really, Venus. We did. I never told you this. Syllie had a little problem. She was in love with you."

"Look," I say sharply, "we came down to this sand-trap countryside to see Acoma. You've pushed me far enough."

"It's true, Venus."

In all these years he has not given me this bulletin. I think I want to kill Philip. "You miserable pimp," I say; and at once I am sorry.

Because Philip always understands. And because Philip is,
and especially was, so beautiful—man-beautiful, Hermes-of-
Praxiteles beautiful, you beautiful dog of a Michelangelic man.
Sometimes I say, "You dog, Philip," but what I mean is not
a big hairy Irish wolfhound but a dog of kings, a runner, with
a big but delicate nose, a bounding white streak on the acres
of a royal park. And how he wags his tail!

Golly, I'm a little tiddly.

Beautiful Philip. On the grass court at the casino that summer, in white flannels—whatever became of the prettiest trousers men ever wore?—and a white shirt with long sleeves, and
tennis shoes chalky with that stuff out of a tube that one put
on (he, Philip, put on every day) with a tiny sponge, a real
sponge out of the Mediterranean Sea, and brand-new white
tennis balls, and point-winning cloudlets of lime flying up
when he uncurled his back and got away one of those spinning
parabolic services of his with the high, kicking bounce; and
rushing the net, bending for a low volley, legs calipered, and
his hair still in place without a lick of bear fat or axle grease
or whatever those gigolos use.

"Why do they say 'love' when you have no points in tennis?
What kind of love is that?"

"Search me why, darling."

"I'd hate to think that I get no points for what I feel about
Meredith." It wasn't Drua's fault. It was our Philip's fault—
your fault, darling. Meredith is mild because he had a fool for
a father. Yes, Philip. They all said it. Skilly said it. Frickie
said it. They said everyone knew you were a damned fool at
the office, and a person who managed the extraordinary feat
of being a fool at Peters, Silliman must have been a fool across
the board. They said that at the office someone always had to
come along behind you and tidy up the mess you'd made of
things: like those London street sweepers—remember that

time?—following behind the procession with the maharajahs riding in the little houses on the backs of elephants, and do you remember the expression on the sweepers' faces when they saw what the collapse of the British Empire was depositing on Regent Street? Oh, God, I'm on the coloreds again. Did we see that thing of the elephants, or was that in a movie? That's the trouble with remembering, Philip: one can't tell anymore what was real in the past. It has all changed so much. Look at this New Type, Pretz, who's actually *running* things at Peters, Silliman nowadays.

"Philip, they'll certify you and lock you up if you propose our Pretzel for the Links Club."

"I don't know, Venus. If he pulls off this merger he's working on, they might consider changing the rules."

"You're a fool."

"Venus!"

Where do I get such evil thoughts? I was always a good girl. Even by then—that summer—that tennis summer—I was still an innocent child. My mother and father had rented a house in Middletown, Rhode Island. Inasmuch as Philip's parents were in the *Social Register*, my parents thought it would be all right for him to visit us for a whole month. He had just graduated from New Haven, his job as a runner wouldn't start until the fall. Perhaps *they*—the old crusts in the big stone mansions—thought us fast. We stayed up "late," we sometimes made a noise driving through town as late as nine at night, but we were pure in heart. Hurt no living creature! Unlike our off-Beat grandson Chum today—a premature adult masquerading as a child—we then were children pretending to be adults. We belonged to Bailey's Beach, but we thought it very superior to swim instead by ourselves on Third Beach, which was deserted. We lolled there looking across

at the Sakonnet lighthouse. We were much too modest to
skinny-dip. I wore wool bathing suits with legs reaching nearly
to my knees. Philip almost never touched me—a few sweet
stolen kisses—because we lived by the code of the time. Neck-
ing wasn't even invented until a decade later. We wouldn't
have dreamed of sleeping with people unless we married them.
Our libidos blew a hot smoke through our bodies, which
sometimes came billowing out of our mouths in the form of
quarrels.

Oh, now a sickening thought: Philip was the one who
wanted to swim on Third Beach. Was it really to "get away
from all those Groton meatballs," or did he know, somewhere
in his mind, that all those others at Bailey's Beach thought
him, even then, a fool? I remember whispers, snickers. At the
time I was somehow able to construe them as the sounds of
envy and admiration. Poor Philip! Poor Philip!

"Remember Third Beach?"

As so often, our responsive Philip answers a question with
a one-upping question. "Remember the telephone pole with
a wagon wheel on top of it, and an osprey nest built there?"

"Philip, why did we swim on Third Beach?"

Philip is silent for a long time; he looks as if he had taken
a sip of coffee that was too hot. Finally: "You and I have always
run away from the crowd, Venus."

Oh, no! I feel honesty sticking in my throat. I don't want
to be like Syllie, inflicting "truth" on the beloved—or even
on myself. For the truth must be that Philip wasn't the only
fool. Another one loved him with a trusting child's open heart.

I feel a stab of "it." I hear barking. "Let's get out of this
damnable North Pole of a bar. I need a hot bath."

"Then we'll have a nice nap, won't we, Venus pie?"

"Don't you use that nurse's 'we' on me, you idiot."

"Venus!"

"I'm sorry, dear Philip. I'm sorry. You've taken me too far

from home. I'm so used up. I yearn for a long long nap in my own bed at 514."

"Never mind, darling. We're going to have dinner abroad. Come along. I'll wake you at eight o'clock."

It is nine-twenty on a rather chilly March evening. Three persons in assorted costumes—two men and a woman—having cleared papers at the Immigration Service shack, start across the bridge. It is an old steel-truss affair with a springtime profusion of blossoms of rust along its beams; it has room for a single file of autos each way; there is very little traffic; an occasional car makes the whole bridge tremble. The three are on a pedestrians' walkway on the right hand as they face Mexico. On the outer side there is a rusty railing, a bit more than waist high, with wire mesh fencing down to the planks of the pathway. The lights of Ciudad Juárez seem to slide sidewise on the sluggish current of the river, the surface of which is perhaps fifteen feet below the feet of the three.

The taller man, on the outside as they walk, is in a white linen suit, and he is wearing immaculate white buckskin shoes. He has on a white shirt and a tie with a subdued Paisley design in which the predominant colors are pale blue and yellow. He has broad shoulders and a rugged build, though he walks with a slight limp. His fluffy brindled brown hair, nowhere thinned, swoops low on his forehead, which therefore seems crowded down through a series of scored crosslines to two prominent bumps looming over full brown eyebrows; his cheeks recede beneath their high bones into hollows and deep lip lines; the chin is firm. This face would be fierce, were it not for the fact that the lights of the Mexican city glisten in decidedly soft brown eyes, which turn frequently toward the face of the woman on his arm.

The other man walks on the traffic side. Short and slight,

he is in a shiny black silk suit, doubtless of Italian manufacture, with padded shoulders which make sharp angles over the sleeves; his necktie screams in a wildly incongruous splash of Marimekko colors. On his tiny feet he has sharply pointed black shoes, so highly polished as to seem to be made of patent leather. He is three-quarters bald, and his pointed face and eggish pate gleam with a tan so deep that it must go right through to the skull. The look of polished mahogany brings the word "magnate" to mind: a powerful creature with a marked talent for vacation. This gent has the ferret eyes of a mind reader. He turns his head nervously this way and that, as if afraid he may miss a trick.

The woman, between the two men, leans on the arm of the one in white. She looks like the ghost of a pirate. She is dressed all in black: black shoes, black slacks, a black sweater, and a wide-brimmed black felt hat, with the left side of the brim turned up to the crown, Aussie or buccaneer style, pinned there with a huge Tiffany gold scarab. A Liberty scarf is loosely tied at her throat, looking as though it might be pulled up over her chin and nose as a piratical disguise, if need should come. Heavy gold bracelets, like a disorderly heap of barrel hoops, pull her thin left arm down straight as a plumb line. The procession of the three has a funerary gravity, because the woman takes very small steps and seems to wait quite a while to gather her resources after each step. To the dim light from the far bank her face offers a memory of great beauty. She carries her chin high; she seems to be sniffing.

"You didn't tell me how *big* the bridge would be," she says to the tall man. The bigness is in the eye of the beholder. It is a small bridge.

The man in white says, "We'll be there before you know it, Venus."

The short man, looking ahead, says, "Jeez, what a mingy town."

"You didn't have to come," the woman sharply says. "Why don't you go back?"

"Now, honey," the tall man says, "be sweet."

"I don't need his complaints tonight. Nothing is ever good enough for him."

"I din't mean anything," the short man says.

"I think all that neon looks sort of cheerful," the tall man says.

"Honky-tonk," the short man says.

The woman takes a labored step. "Pretzel," she says, "would you try to make the supreme sacrifice, and be still? Please don't speak. I want to be with Philip."

"My lips are sealed, dolling."

Two steps require concentration. "Philip, why didn't you think to bring my lifesaver? You know they'll have hard wooden seats in this country we're going to."

"Would you like me to go back and get it?"

"I would not like you to go back and get it. I would like the Pretz to go back and get it."

The short man says, "How can I say I'll be glad to get it without speaking?"

The man in white gives the short man a set of car keys.

"Excuse all the talk," the short man says, "but where will I meet you?"

The woman says, "Don't worry, we'll still be on this endless bridge."

"We'll wait for you," the tall man says. "Thanks, old boy."

The short man walks back to North America.

The tall man and the woman stand still for a long time. The woman is looking up at the man's face, with the look of a votary unsure of her faith. "My good friend," she says, her head canted by her obvious emotion toward the man's shoulder. Then, after a pause, "Where did we go wrong?"

"Wrong?"

But she doesn't explain what she has meant. She throws all of herself into taking a step. "I'm so cold," she says.

"Was this a mistake, Venus? Should we go back?"

"There is no way of going back."

"When Pretz comes—"

But she doesn't answer. She takes two steps. Then, halted, she says, "There was one spring when I couldn't bear to be indoors—remember, darling? The shadblow was out. A blue-bird nested on the power-line pole at the west stone wall. The woodchuck was always after the clover at the end of the field. Buckie—the best Lab we ever had—ran away every day to see his friends. Meredith picked me some violets. The terrace of the lawn was finally almost clear of dandelions, I *hated* dandelions. The forsythia held on for the longest time. I remember waiting for the glossy leaves of the franklinia to come out—it was always last. The lettuce was up in the garden, the peas of course were up, but no sign yet of asparagus. Remember that owl that hooted in the pines? That spring?"

"I'm not sure which spring you mean, Venus."

"There. You see. Which spring. Ah, Philip, where did we go wrong?"

"Now, honey, cheer up. We'll have some nice hot Mexican food."

One step. Another step. "Meredith owes me something more than violets," the woman says.

"Did you lend him money, Venus? That was imprudent."

"I don't *mean* money. You have a mind like a safe."

"Oh," the man says, "I see what you mean. You mean—that business of tennis points? But honey, I'm afraid we never can collect debts of that kind."

"Not till too late. He'll want to pay. Merri keeps a very tidy checkbook, he'll want to remit. It'll be too late. He'll be sorry. It'll ruin his life."

The woman's sniffing is more definite now. She is shivering.

She says: "You pick this time to tell me that Syllie had a sn-sn-sneaker for me."

"It was more than that."

"Philip, I adjure you to tell me the truth. Did you have one for her? She'd scream if you touched her. Was *that* the allure?"

"Venus, you're behaving in a very peculiar way."

"I know I am. Are we halfway across the bridge? Have we crossed the border?"

"Almost. Not quite."

She takes three steps, rather quicker than any of her previous steps. She seems to be having some difficulty breathing; it is as if she were climbing a steep hill.

"I want a little rest," she says. "Let's stand here a minute." She moves toward the railing and leans on it. She gazes down at the dark river. "I adored looking down from the upper decks, watching the spume go by."

"Venus, there was never anyone important but you."

"I know, Philip. Thank you, Philip. Let's go on now to the border."

"I don't know whether it's marked."

"*You*'ll want to pay, too, Philip, but it will be too late for you, too." The woman's breath catches, and the man looks sharply at her.

"Venus, are you all right?"

"The unimportances add up to importance, don't they? I was bad to you, too, you know."

"You're trembling, dear heart. Let's go back."

"I wish we could, Philip."

She takes a false step. It is as if one knee were rubbery. She lifts her head, and she takes several firm steps. Considering her previous pace, it is as if she were running.

"Whoa, Venus," the man says, "this is the middle of the bridge."

The woman takes three more steps, evidently to place herself for a certainty in alien territory. In the half-light one can see a change in her face. Is she smiling? "It always takes so long," she says in a weak voice.

"What did you say?"

"I said, 'How divine.' "

Suddenly her legs give out, and before the man in white can react, she is sitting on the planks of the walkway. At this very moment, the short man comes along at a quick pace, with the circular rubber tube under his arm. "Jeez," he says, "is she crocked?"

"Venus," the tall man says, leaning down over her, "I don't think we can sit here."

She is panting, but he can make out her slowly spoken words: "I'm going to wait here in the salon, until the lighter comes alongside."

The man in white makes a signal to the short man, who hands over the rubber ring. The tall man puts it on the planks behind the woman. Each man reaches under an armpit, and they lift the woman a few inches, the tall man pushes the ring under her with his foot, and they gently let her down.

"Go back to the customs shed and ask for an American doctor. The last thing she needs is a Mex at this point."

The short man runs. The man in white leans down, and he hears the woman groan.

"Oh, God," she distinctly says, "I knew it would be a dog."

"We'll have you in bed in a jiffy, Venus," the man says.

Her lips are moving, she is mumbling.

The man spreads a handkerchief and kneels on it on one white knee and puts his ear near her mouth. "Say it again, Venus."

He hears her. "Darling . . . tell Drua . . ."

The Blouse

After Myra had her baby, she used to take the infant to the post office to get the clerk, Mr. Fleming, to weigh it for her because she had no scales. One day she was in a bad mood. She asked Mr. Fleming, "How much would it cost to mail her to California, parcel post?"

Mr. Fleming put the baby on the scales. "Wouldn't you want to send her special handling?" he asked.

"Not today I wouldn't."

The baby was blithely kicking its legs and waving its arms, so the needle on the scales must have wobbled. Mr. Fleming, leaning forward to concentrate on it, tightened his lips and pushed his glasses up the ridge of his nose with his little finger. "Nine dollars and seventy-eight cents," he finally said.

"Imagine it," she said. "If I just had a friend out there on the West Coast, I'd be tempted. Today I would."

Mr. Fleming handed the baby back across the counter. "Have a good day, Mistress Myra," he said, and nodded to the next in line.

Myra tucked the baby into the canvas sling on her chest and stepped out into the bright noon. The air was still. This was one of those August days on the Vineyard when the sky is like a huge flat hunk of beach glass, milky and baked hot by the sun. The flowers in the beds in front of the post office drooped from a long drought. The loudspeaker at the ferry parking lot suddenly crackled and a voice with an impatient edge shouted, "Standby drivers report to your cars! All standby drivers report to your cars immediately." Myra thought, If only I were a traveler, I'd drive like the wind. Somewhere, somewhere. The baby squirmed and kicked in the snug sling as if it were still in Myra's belly. Myra walked across Five Corners through disorderly traffic, certain that no driver would run down a mother carrying an infant. And what if one did? Safely across, she realized that she had forgotten to ask Mr. Fleming how much the baby weighed, and she said, "Damn." But she didn't feel like going back.

At the A & P she laid the baby down on the bottom of a shopping cart, with the sling for a pillow, and she pushed slowly up and down the aisles. The air-conditioning felt good. She took her time. She put a box of Pampers down in the cart beside the baby. It was gurgling with joy, seeming to see divinity in the fitful flickering of the neon lights up above. "My God," Myra said, appalled at its senseless happiness. She tucked around the baby a jar of peanut butter, a loaf of Wonder bread, a bag of Doritos, a packet of hot dogs, some dill pickles, a box of spinach spaghetti, a container of whole milk, and a frozen pizza. Waiting her turn at a checkout slot, she picked two Milky Ways off a rack and read the headlines on the *Enquirer*.

Her turn came. As she lifted her purchases up onto the movable platform, she wondered what stupid thing this check-out girl—a new one to her—would say about the baby. They always said, " 'ook at the 'ittle w'inkles on its w'ist," or, when the baby had nothing on but diapers, they would lean over and poke a finger in its belly button and sing, "Ding-a-ling!" But this one was having a hard time finding the right numbers to push on the cash register. She was a fat girl with short hair, which was bleached white on the tips and stood up in little spikes. Her lower lip hung loose, weighed down by the density of her confusion. After a while she shouted, "Mrs. Watson!"

The supervisor came over. She was a friend of Myra's mother, a goodhearted woman but a terrible gossip. She was thin and walked with both shoulders pushed forward. She said, "Good morning, Myra dear."

Myra said, "I wish it was good."

The checkout girl said, "I never can remember . . . the subtotal gizmo . . . which one."

Mrs. Watson gave Myra a look, as if to confide, These checkout morons I have to put up with. Myra didn't specially want to be on her side. "ST for subtotal, dear. Right in front of your nose."

"Jeez," the girl said, and punched the button.

Myra wondered why this kind of thing always happened to her. No one else seemed to get stuck in the checkout slots. The baby was impatient, too. It had stopped gurgling; in a minute it would be howling.

"I can't get over that cat of your mother's," Mrs. Watson said to Myra. "The way it sits up there on the TV, won't look at you, faces away from you, you know. And then it lashes its tail back and forth across the screen. I said to your mother the other day—well, first of all I have to tell you, when I drop in on her, she'll flick her little remote gadget, put the sound on mute, you know, but she keeps the picture going, and she keeps looking at it while you're talking with her, as if she's fitting *your* words onto the pictures—so as I was leaving the other day I said to her, 'Ethel, dear,' I said, 'do you want me to take the cat down?' You know what she says? She barks at me, real mad. 'Not *yet*,' she says. So I just left. Sometimes I wonder."

This was one morning when Myra didn't want to have a conversation about her mother. She just grunted and bagged the things.

"Twenty-six dollars thirty-one cents," the girl said.

"It couldn't be," Myra said.

Mrs. Watson poked a hand around in Myra's two bags and said, "She's right. You'll have to ring up again."

"This is not my day," the dumb girl said.

"Look who's talking," Myra said. She tucked the baby back in the sling.

The total turned out to be sixteen dollars and thirty-one cents.

Myra said to the girl, "Do they train you to slip in an extra ten now and then, so they'll make more money? Do you get a commission for extra tens?"

"Why, Myra," Mrs. Watson said, "I'm surprised at you."

"Sometimes I'm surprised at myself," Myra said. "You can tell Mom that, next time you see her."

As she left the store, she felt rotten about the way she'd spoken to the girl and to Mrs. Watson. The girl must be what? A junior in high school? I'm only a couple of years older than her, Myra thought, and I'm no better. I have to be stupider. Look where I've got myself. She walked up toward Main Street. Her legs hurt, going uphill, what with the weight of the baby and the two grocery bags, one under each arm. The baby fell asleep, and its head began bouncing against her chest with each step she took. Myra thought that if only she could cry, she'd be better off, but somewhere along the way she'd lost the use of tears.

She crossed Main Street and stopped to look in the window of the Thrift Shop. A big Japanese kimono was hanging there, and Myra remembered a photograph she had seen once, of a Japanese woman deferentially walking along three paces behind her husband. She felt a stab of anger. Then she thought, God,

I've got to put these packages down. I'll buy myself something
to wear—that always makes me feel better.

She walked into the shop and around to the glass counter
on the left. She was glad to see Samantha Burrow at the cash
register. Samantha's face was half again as wide as anyone
needed, her eyes were far apart, and her mouth was like a
metal letter slot at the post office, but Myra thought her lovely.
Some kind of survivor's beauty came out from inside her. She
was the daughter of summer people from out on West Chop,
heavy drinkers; she was living on the island all year now, she
didn't want to be rich, she was a totally natural person—calm
and kind and willing to listen. It figured that she would be
a volunteer at the Thrift Shop.

"Can I park these groceries here for a minute?" Myra asked.

"Only if you'll let me hold the baby while you look around,"
Samantha said.

"You got it," Myra said, and she handed the baby over,
waking it up in the process. She put the sling on the counter,
beside the brown-paper bags.

Samantha made cooing noises. The baby screwed up its face
to cry, but then changed its mind and fell asleep again, its
cheek against Samantha's breast.

Myra felt at home in the Thrift Shop, among all the objects
that people hadn't wanted to keep. First she drifted along by
the lengthy display of chinaware and glasses and bits of bric-
a-brac; some people might have said that these amounted to
a lot of tacky junk, but Myra felt a sweet harmony in all the
abandoned things. At the back of the store, next to the shelves
of outgrown toys, there was a disturbing jumble of discards
that hadn't yet been sorted and tagged for display, which
seemed to have been thrown in a heap in anger. She crossed
cautiously—because she only had a few dollars on her—toward
the racks of women's clothing. As she went past the rows of
dresses and pants, she put out her hand, now and then, just

to touch. She was drawn toward the blouses. Grasping the hangers, she pressed this blouse and that one back against its neighbors to check it over, and suddenly she felt desperately lonely, sensing the crowd of women on whose shoulders these pieces of clothing had not seemed comfortable or pretty enough. Then she saw a blouse she loved. It was a pale, pale saffron color, simply cut, slightly fitted, with a tricot collar. She had a vague feeling she had seen it on someone and had thought that person beautiful. She took it over and held it up for Samantha to see.

Samantha said, "Cool, Myra. How about bartering? The blouse in exchange for this lousy bundle, huh? Oooooh!" She squeezed the baby.

"You're not far off," Myra said.

The blouse cost four dollars. Myra stuffed it in one of the A & P bags. She felt better till she realized she had to walk all the way up to Greenwood and then over to Franklin to get home—if home was what you could call those two miserable little rooms her mother had rented for her at the rear of Mrs. Wickham's house. By the time she got there, her legs and shoulders and arms all felt numb.

She went around to the back of the house and pushed the door open with her shoulder. At once she heard her mother's voice, beyond the door, saying, "Darling, I wish you'd lock up. On these back streets. You never know, even Vineyard Haven these days."

"Oh, Mom, thank God you're here. Would you take these things? . . . You wouldn't be in here if I locked up. You'd have had to go on home."

"I know, but I worry, darling," Myra's mother said. She leaned the broom she was holding against a wall and took the bags from Myra, one at a time, setting them on the small table at the center of the room. Myra saw that her mother had been picking up. She had washed the dishes from the night before and from breakfast, and now she'd been sweeping the floor. Myra thought, This is supposed to be my house.

"Ah, look at ums," her mother said. "Isn't ums sweet?"

"No, she's not sweet. She stinks."

"Do you want me to change her?"

"Mom, that's so hypocritical. You know changing her makes you nauseous."

Myra put the baby on the drainboard by the sink, fetched the Pampers from one of the A & P bags, opened the box, and undressed the baby. Unable to watch, her mother went to the window. Myra cleaned the baby's bottom with a rag and warm water from the sink faucet, dried the round places and all the little creases, shook powder on, snapped a new diaper in place, and then sat down in a wooden rocker in a corner. She hummed and rocked.

"I've just come from the hospital," her mother said. "I have bad news. Mabel—Mrs. Stritch, you know?—from Tashmoo Avenue?—Dr. Branford opened her up and found a huge big cancer in her stomach. I got talking with Mrs. Darkin, the nurse in the waiting room. She said what they took out, it was just like a big bunch of grapes. There wasn't anything to do but sew her up again. I'll miss her so."

"She isn't dead yet, Mom."

The baby, dry and clean, had begun to chirp like a sparrow.

"Mrs. Darkin said there was no use even giving her a prognosis. Sometimes I think I'd like to be a Christian Scientist."

"What are you saying?"

"For one thing, I wouldn't have to worry about doctors' bills anymore. I wouldn't have to pay for Blue Cross. And anyways, it's all in the mind, you know."

"Mother, don't you dare. I hate to say it, but you're getting on. Listen to these stories you keep telling me, about all your friends with embolisms and pancreatitis and malignant thises and thats. If you stop Blue Cross and get sick, that'd be one more thing on my back. To pay the bills you'd talked yourself out of."

"And where would you get the money?"

And so, Myra thought, Mom has worked her way around to him again. Look at her eyes soften, and that hurt look. She loves me so much that she'd like to murder me. Myra tore her eyes away from her mother's face and looked down at the baby. It had its mouth open, and its tongue was lolling out and back, and its ravishing dark brown eyes, with little distorted rectangles of window light laid out on them, seemed groggy with contentment. Myra thought angrily, Why can't anyone around here feel what I feel? "Where would I get the money?" she asked with heavy irony. "Hey, Mom, that's the best question you ever asked."

"Oh, honey, he'll be back. You watch. After Labor Day, after all those pretty high-toned off-island waitresses go back to college, he'll come back to you with his tail between his legs."

"And his wallet full of money in his back pocket, I suppose. I don't want him back."

"Mylie! Mylie! You know you do."

"I do not. I hate him. You tricked me."

"I tricked you? How? You mean, into marrying him? Excuse me, darling, but what is that you're holding in your arms? You do have a baby, you know. That's the one and only reason you got married."

"It's your fault I have this stupid baby. It's your fault. You said you'd shoot me before you'd let me get rid of it."

"Myra, did I fill myself up with beer night after night and crawl in the back seat of his father's Chevrolet with a selfish high-school boy? Did I? Let's not talk fault, Myra."

"And *his* shitty mother. You would have to go to her and spill the whole thing, and she would have to go to the priest, and—"

The baby had begun to whoop with joy. "Yawp!" it said. Its eyes blazed. "Wah!"

"You were always such a good girl, Mylie, you were always so decent, so kind, so obedient, what happened? It gives me the shudders to hear you use words like that. Mrs. Thirrup is a wonderful woman."

"Don't say 'Thirrup.' I hate that name."

"It's yours now, dear."

There was a silence then as mother and daughter both drew back from what they had been saying and thinking. Myra's anger seeped quickly away. She felt as if nothing strong held on in her anymore. She glanced down at the baby and saw that for the first time in its life it was looking deeply into her eyes. My God, she thought, she wants to know if I'm going to do her someday the way Mom does me.

Her mother softly said, "Can I make you a cup of tea, honey?"

Myra sighed. "Why don't you fix us some hot dogs? I just got some new ones in one of those bags."

"No, darling, I can't stay. I promised Helen I'd be over. I told you about her knee with the fluid in it. I'll set some water on for tea."

"It's okay," Myra said. "It's okay. I can eat later."

Her mother left. Myra sat there quite a while. Then she took the baby into the bedroom, where she saw that her mother had made the bed. She put the baby down on it and went back to take the groceries out of the bags. As she picked the first bag up to fold it, she saw that her mother had tucked two twenty-dollar bills under it. She put them in the pocket of her jeans. The blouse was on top in the other bag. She held it up to the light by the shoulders and decided to try it on.

She went in the bedroom, took off her shirt and her nursing bra, and threw them on the bed beside the baby. She put on the blouse and buttoned it up. She opened the bathroom door, turned on the overhead light, and looked at herself in the mirror over the basin.

At once she realized who it was she'd seen in the blouse and thought so beautiful. Herself. "My God," she said out loud, "I'm buying stuff from the Thrift Shop that I sold them. And I thought that girl in the A & P was dumb." She remembered the anger, months ago, when she knew she was pregnant and had taken the blouse to the shop to get rid of it. Yet now she felt the best she'd felt all day. She was pleased by what she saw in the mirror. It was a neat blouse, and with her figure now she looked real good. She crossed her arms with her hands on her shoulders. The fabric was so nice and soft. She closed her eyes. She remembered the light touch of his fingers slowly undoing the buttons that first night, beginning at the top. One by one. No hurry. One at a time. "God damn it!" she shouted, and she left the bathroom and slammed its door.

That started the baby crying. In a few moments it was tuned up to a sustained screaming, holding its breath and turning purple. When the baby was mad it looked like him. Everyone said it looked like him. Myra picked the baby up and took it in the kitchen. She settled in the rocker, facing the window, but rocking did no good. The little body was as hard as wood. The outcry came in gasps. "It's okay," Myra said, just as she had said to her mother. "It's okay." Then, in a kind of daydream, she started undoing the buttons with delicate care. She took her time. One by one. Like on those nights. When the buttons were all unbuttoned at last, she folded back the left side of the blouse and gave her breast to her child.

The eager mouth took the bud and tugged at it in a rage of need. In a matter of moments, the hard little back eased itself into a curve, the hands came unclenched and brushed the breast with a light touch, and the cheeks faded from purple to a creamy pink. Myra felt a warmth in her chest as the mother milk flowed, and when she looked down at the silky fuzz of an eyebrow and the unbelievable upsweep of lashes that she could just barely see, the warmth spread farther, and even her hands and feet began to tingle.

She raised her eyes to the window, and she saw the world. Slivers of dazzling light, slanting from right to left, winked on the leathery leaves of the oaks and were combed by the needles on the pines. Splashes of brilliance washed the trunks. The old pines had bark like alligator hide. She'd never noticed. There was moss on the shady side of the oaks. Then all the radiance out there began to shimmer at the edges, and Myra knew that no words had ever been made up to tell about what she could see just then.

Without lowering her eyes, she lifted the right side of the blouse and covered her daughter's legs.

The Announcement

"Mother's a bit old-fashioned," Gordon said. In spite of his confidence in Beverly, he couldn't help feeling apprehensive about this first meeting. "Still wears hairpins, you know. I think they're made of deer horn. She winds a braid around on top like a crown."

"You don't have to . . . p-paint her," Bev said. "I'm going to see her with my own eyes, right? How much f-farther?"

"We're not far now. Just the other side of Pleasantville."

He left the exact distance hanging. In a moderate hurry, he kept the rented Skylark ticking along at sixty. Beverly looked just right to him. She was all in black, in an off-the-shoulder taffeta cocktail dress, with a triangular black silk shawl, knotted in front, so that there were only glimpses of skin. Bev's instincts were so unerring: his mother often chose black herself for cheerful occasions. Beverly's curly dark hair was blowing in the breeze from her half-opened window. She had understated her makeup that morning—how much she understood!

Gordon was especially nervous because his mother's Thanksgiving dinner had had to be postponed by a day. As usual, brother Peter, coming from Minneapolis with his family, had made a mess of things; there had been some kind of slipup with their train reservations. Gordon knew that his mother, with her great gift of denial, would sit through the meal in style and wouldn't show a single outward sign of distress. But Thanksgiving dinner on the day after!

Thanksgiving meant everything to his mother. The resilience of the New England settlers was in her arteries—the grit and bend of those forebears, who could survive a first blizzardy winter, scrape at hardscrabble soil in a thin spring, plant a fish head in every corn hill, pray away drought and the crashing down of hailstones, and, at last, stack the surviving stalks and roll in the huge pumpkins and shoot a wild turkey, and then feast, and murmur in gratitude to a jealous God. That Puritan side was only a part of her, though. She was, as well, a sensuous family woman, and Thanksgiving dinners were her joy and her victory. As children, Gordon and his brother Peter had basked in the sunlight of her nurture: strange to think of that hot motherly effulgence, because she so liked shadowy places and somber clothes. She had devoted herself to her husband—dead now ten years—with a quirky tenderness that had some cold spots in it. She had quarreled with him often, perhaps to starch up a certain rumpled softness in him, and Gordon had come to see that she had always lost the arguments but had somehow won by losing.

This mysterious femininity, yielding yet powerful, Victorian yet Emersonian too, had been what Gordon had looked for in a wife the first time, when he came back from the war in the South Pacific; but marrying an apparent clone of his mother hadn't worked. Sue hadn't turned out to fit the mold, and Gordon and she had had a rough parting, four years ago, in the autumn when Eisenhower beat Stevenson for the second time. No kids, thank goodness. Badly burned, he had gone it alone for three and a half years, and then had fallen in love with this complicated Beverly, who was not in the least like his mother. He and Bev had long since decided to marry, but for some reason—perhaps it was because Bev was fourteen years younger than he—he had postponed bringing her to meet his mother until now, on the special occasion of a Thanksgiving dinner, when, he thought, his mother's euphoria, as well as the sweet condiments in little bowls on her table (Beverly had a sugar-tooth), might ease the way on both sides. "Bev has a funny little stammer," he had said to his mother on the phone after accepting for both of them, as if that would explain all about Beverly in advance.

As they approached Chappaqua, Gordon's familiarity since childhood with the shapes of the hills thereabouts, his memory of each rough-cut stone bridge on the parkway, his long acquaintance even with certain noble trees along the road, especially some of the huge willows in the low places—first of all flora to put out yellowy growth in the spring, last of all to trail their drying yellowy feathers in the fall—these mnemonics of homing stirred up in his senses a rush of remembered small pleasures: the sight of his mother unwrapping a stick of butter and leaning down to let Barabbas, the old Lab, lick the traces off the wax paper; the taste of cinnamon toast; diving into huge piles of leaves when his father raked them up on Saturday afternoons in the fall; deep sounds, of cello and bassoon, on the Capehart; the gentle sidling of Whitefoot, the only cat he'd ever liked, snaking against his calf with a flirtatious aftertouch of her tail. All the years. He drove with care.

Then they were there. "Good God," Beverly said when they drove up under the darkness of the porte cochere. Gordon laughed. Yes, the house was a beast. Heavy-timbered, mouse-colored, surrounded by huge red maples which even with bared limbs fought off most of the afternoon's hazy light, the house loomed as a reminder of an era of aspiration and complacency that was, thank heavens, long gone. This monument to Daddy—Gordon called his father that—was planted in that purportedly tranquil zone, discovered by self-made men in the nineteen-twenties, of the one-hour commute to town on the Harlem Division of the New York Central. Never mind. To Gordon, at thirty-eight, it was still home.

Gordon gave one rap on the cast-iron knocker—a head, was it Samson's or a human-looking lion's?—and opened up the heavy door, which squealed its welcome on its long black strap hinges. He waved Bev in ahead of him. Here came Uncle Solbert and his wife, hurrying in good manners out of the living room to greet the newcomers.

"Gordie boy!" Uncle Solbert roared with a second-drink cordiality. Did Gordon remember that Uncle Bert was partial to old-fashioneds?

"Happy Thanksgiving," Aunt Beth cried, already all too happy herself. She, too. Apparently everyone was going to pretend that they had gathered on the right day.

"This is Beverly Zimmer," Gordon said. Bev was blinking. Gordon saw that she had forgotten to straighten her blown hair. She looked wild. The delicate wrinkles in her forehead showed up as she stood right under the down-pouring light of the hall ceiling fixture.

Now all the others, except for Gordon's mother, came rushing into the hall in a stampede of curiosity. Here were brother Peter and his Molly, not the least bit shamefaced. Introductions kept Gordon busy. Here were his mother's ancient dear friends, Miss Rankin and Miss Alderhoff. And here was Mr. Cannahan. Mr. Cannahan's eyes did a little dance when he saw Beverly's shawl slip to one side as she shook hands. "How beautiful," he murmured. And here was awful Freddie, Peter and Molly's son; was he still at Lawrenceville, or had he been kicked out? And sullen little niece Caroline, who, Gordon noticed, had remarkable breasts for—what was she?—a thirteen-year-old?

"Where's Mom?"

"K-k-k-Katy, in the k-kitchen," sang Uncle Solbert, off-key. Gordon felt a hot blush rise up his neck to his cheeks. His mother obviously hadn't passed on the little secret about Bev.

But there she came. His mother was wearing a charcoal-gray dress, which was almost entirely hidden by a wraparound blue apron. She had something in a dish in her hand. Her piercing dark eyes were looking not at him but at Beverly, and he was astonished by the sharp pang of joy and pride he felt when he saw the genuine warmth in the gathers of crow's feet—the smile lines—around his mother's eyes. She went straight to Beverly and, holding the dish out to one side, leaned forward and kissed her, but really kissed her, not just the air beside her cheek, and spoke a single word, "Beverly."

Beverly took a step backward and said, "I'm so . . . t-tickled to meet you." At once she had offered Gordon's mother the tiny hesitation and catch that he found so entrancing: a pause, as verbal choices came to her, and then a little splutter of emotion, tripping over a plosive consonant, as she settled on a word that sounded a bit odd but must have been, as usual, exactly what she meant.

Gordon's mother greeted him with a tight one-armed hug and then turned at once and hurried back to the kitchen, holding the dish high in her right hand to show the company why she was in such haste. Everyone drifted back to the living room. As they walked in, Gordon heard music coming from the old Capehart. Sibelius's Seventh. Ah, yes, one of his mother's favorites, that swooping deep-toned utterance, sad as whale song, from a country where for months the sun never came up over the horizon. Yet the sound was part of what made Gordon's spirits rise; it belonged, as he did, in this room, with its dark mahogany wainscoting and twisted black ironwork fireplace tools and mock-candle sconces holding tiny, dim, flame-shaped light bulbs; all those things were embedded in, and had somehow failed to darken, his makeup. Bev's face, as he quickly checked it now, reinforced his pleasure. Her eyes were twinkling at the sights in the room—that the look might contain elements of ambiguity: delight yet at the same time something like disbelief?

He saw that a bar had been set up on the old tea wagon in the corner of the room. "Have a Thanksgiving libation?" he quietly asked Bev.

"You can bet your . . . b-bottom dollar I will," she said. She surprised him by asking for gin and bitters. She usually sipped Dubonnet or Cinzano.

"Did you see that Macy's had a huge toy elephant in their parade?" he heard Miss Rankin say as he crossed to the tea wagon. The Persian rug he walked over was worn down to the warp in the trafficway from the hall and in front of several chairs.

"I wonder if those gigantic balloons in the parade aren't dangerous," Miss Alderhoff said. "I mean, if it's windy."

"There's wasn't a breath of air yesterday," Aunt Beth said, and then she laughed hard, having given a little too much emphasis, Gordon thought, to "yesterday."

Leaning over the bar, looking for the gin, Gordon saw a bottle of amontillado with a little cardboard tag hung around its neck on a slip of ribbon. Looking more closely, he read the words written in his mother's hand on the tag:

BEST SHERRY
DO NOT USE

He would wait and see whether to tell Bev about that. He mixed her drink—he found bitters in a tiny square cruet—and shook up a manhattan for himself.

With his arrival in his mother's house he felt it proper that he should take over from Peter, two years his junior, the duties of a host, and when he had given Beverly her drink, he turned and said, "Anyone else? Mr. Cannahan?"

"Oh, *no*, thank you," Mr. Cannahan said, tearing his eyes away from the tantalizing knot that held Beverly's shawl in place, and rubbing his stomach to remind Gordon of the ulcer he had harbored there for so many, many years.

"Of course," Gordon said, remembering. "Forgive me. Beth? Pete? You ready?"

"I can get our own," Peter said.

Gordon sat down. He heard a thunking sound as the Capehart turned a record over. Then the dark Finnish keening resumed.

"And what do you do, Miss Swimmer?" Mr. Cannahan asked.

"Zimmer," Bev said sharply.

"Ah, Miss Zimmer," Mr. Cannahan said. "Lovely name."

"I do . . . n-nothing," Beverly said.

"Best occupation in the world!" Uncle Solbert shouted.

Gordon was trying to think of something sensible to say when his mother came into the room and took a chair. She had removed her apron. "Dear me," she said. "Such confusion. Flo says she'll be ready to serve in five minutes."

"What nice earrings," Beverly said, to Gordon's delight. She was going to be wonderful.

Gordon's mother put her hands over the amber pendants at her ears. "They hurt," she said. "But do you know? I had a brainstorm. I put Dr. Scholl's corn plasters on the screw pads. Perfect!"

"Perfect" was a word his mother often used, with an ever-so-slight Englishy softening of the *r*. She posted many little signs and notices around the house, like the tag on the sherry bottle, and Gordon thought of the one that used to be stuck beside the shower handle in the guest bathroom: FOR BEST SHOWERBATH, TURN TO TEN O'CLOCK. WAIT 45 SECONDS. PERFECT! But she was far from being a perfectionist; nor, Gordon had long since acknowledged, was she herself perfect.

He sometimes thought that she considered one's manner of speaking more important than what one said. A person's emotional tone, a person's feeling toward her, toward the world, was what counted with her. Sometimes she nattered, rattled on without hearing herself. She was kind and warm, though, and always wanted to boost other people's morale. He remembered how, when Daddy was alive, she used to sound off about his being the big man around the place. "The eye of the owner is good for the land," she would say. Her George was "the only man on the island." Yet she had that appetite for quarrels. She often accused her husband, in front of the boys—absurdly, Gordon thought—of letting other women flirt with him. Not of his having flirted himself. She asked friends what was troubling them, really dug out the dirt; she wanted to sympathize, wanted to help, wanted to be loved for being loving. This last craving had sometimes struck Gordon, especially when he had troubles of his own, as a need for something much less adorable than it might seem—a need for some kind of firm grip on your arm. The miracle, though, was her persistent cheerfulness since Daddy's death. She seemed not to have a trouble in the world. Thinking of her now, Gordon had a sudden vivid and very happy memory of hot chocolate, French bread, honey.

He looked at Bev. She was smiling. She had loved that thing of the earlobe remedy. Her hair was still a mess. It didn't matter. The emotional tone was what mattered.

Flo, the cook, appeared in the archway from the hall and shouted, "All right, Mrs. Bronson!" Flo was a New England woman; she had her ways.

Brother Peter was the first to stand up. All his life, Peter had been hungry. "Come on, folks," he said. "Get your trotters in the trough."

Gordon went over and turned the Capehart off, and then he offered the crook of his arm to his mother. Taking it, she smiled at him and said, "I want you to carve, son."

Everyone exclaimed at the sight of the table. Glass and silver winked in the afternoon light. Between two newly polished silver candelabra, each bearing five lighted candles of a garish red, stood a display, looking like fireworks bursting in air, of odd varieties of late autumn's greatest pride, the chrysanthemum. Pairs of bottles of red and white wine and two carafes of sweet cider stood on silver circlets on a tablecloth with beautiful doilies of Devonshire lace scattered about. At each place, next to a pale blue napkin folded to stand up, lay one of those crepe-paper tubes for children's parties with tabs to pull from the ends which make a little firecracker sound—each doubtless containing a colored paper hat and a favor of some kind. Strewn here and there were gravy boats and bowls brimming with all the things that Gordon had known Bev would love: watermelon-rind pickles, tomato marmalade, peach chutney, quince jelly, spiced Jerusalem artichokes, green-tomato mincemeat, and, of course, loads of cranberry sauce.

Gordon's mother seated everyone. Gordon at the head of the table, herself at the other end. She put Peter at her right, and Mr. Cannahan at her left. Beverly was between Mr. Cannahan and Uncle Solbert; both men beamed at their luck. The others were scattered around. Gordon had Aunt Beth on his right and Molly on his left.

When they were all seated, Gordon's mother tinkled her wineglass with a knife, and after she had complete silence she said, "Peter, dear, would you say grace, please?" This was evenhanded: Gordon would carve, Peter would pray—a special privilege at Thanksgiving dinner.

"God in heaven," Peter said, with his head down and his eyes squeezed tight shut, "we thank you for this wonderful American tradition, we are grateful for prosperity and our mother's good health, we thank you for family values"—Gordon thought he heard awful little Freddie give a tiny grunt at that —"and the heritage of freedom you have granted our nation. And thanks, by the way, for the turkey-lurkey."

During this performance, Gordon had not bowed his head; he had watched Beverly. She had not lowered her head either but had stared at Peter with a look that gave Gordon a little twinge of concern. But then she laughed with everyone else at Peter's nonsense at the end, and when Uncle Bert started clapping, she joined in with the rest. Peter, acknowledging the applause, clasped his hands above his head, like the winner of a gold medal.

Flo came in, her face pink, her hair flying every which way, and her apron splashed with gravy, carrying a huge, glistening turkey up at a level with her head, and now everyone both clapped and cheered. She put the bird down in front of Gordon and stood there gloating at it.

"What's in the stuffing, Flo?" Uncle Solbert called out when the hubbub died down.

"Well, now, there's chestnuts, and country sausage—that's the thing!—onions, celery, let's see, thyme, sage, bread crumbs, of course, stale bread crumbs. And," she added, with a little lurch in her stance, "perhaps I shouldn't say, folks, but there's Madeira wine in there!" And she went off to the kitchen, cackling.

Picking up the carving knife, Gordon glanced at Beverly. She was looking at him. Her face was glowing. He stood up, took some passes, which he hoped looked skillful, with the knife-edge at the sharpening rod. He leaned forward to start his work.

While he carved, Flo brought in one dish after another, setting each down with a decisive little bang on a doily on the tablecloth, alongside serving spoons that were already dis-

persed there, and announcing each as she put it in place:
mashed potatoes, both white and sweet, in separate casseroles,
with browned marshmallows on top of the latter; oysters in
cornmeal hasty pudding; cut green beans with rosemary;
creamed onions; mushrooms braised with sorrel leaves; baked
turnips flavored with maple syrup.

Waiting to be served, people pulled favor-crackers with their
neighbors, and exclaimed cheerfully at the cheap things they
found inside. Mr. Cannahan and Uncle Bert had a brief tiff
about who would get to pull Beverly's cracker; Uncle Bert
won by sheer force of the bourbon in his veins. He let Beverly
pull Mr. Cannahan's cracker, though. Uncle Bert was the only
one at the table to put on a crepe-paper hat. It was bright
orange. Everyone was talking at once.

Flo brought in Mr. Cannahan's lunch: two bananas, mashed
with a fork into a pulp on a plate. It was all his ulcer was
going to allow him to eat. A general cry of commiseration
went up, but Mr. Cannahan, looking right at Bev, called out,
"I don't mind: it's the company that matters on holidays, isn't
it?"

"You're a good sport," Gordon's mother said, patting Mr.
Cannahan's hand.

There was great confusion while the plates went around
and volunteers served things up in passing. "Light or dark?"
Gordon kept calling out to various customers. The teenager
Caroline couldn't make up her mind. She threw a beseeching
glance at her mother, looking as if she might break into
tears.

"You like white, honey," Molly said.

"I don't either," Caroline said.

"Suit yourself, kiddo," Molly said. "It's your funeral."

Gordon put a helping of both on Caroline's plate, and she
flashed him an angry look.

At last things settled down. Gordon could sit. His back

hurt a little from leaning over, but he felt important. He saw that Beverly had chosen red wine. People were tucking into their food, and for a while the room was quiet.

Then old Miss Rankin and old Miss Alderhoff started the ball rolling.

"Wasn't it sweet," Miss Rankin said, "that Jackie Kennedy had her baby on Thanksgiving night?"

"I was so offended," Miss Alderhoff said, "that AP fellow trying to take Mrs. Kennedy's picture on the way back from the delivery room. Is there no privacy in this world anymore? I mean to say, the President-elect's wife!"

"Another John Fitzgerald Kennedy, did you see what they're naming him?" Peter said with his mouth full. "Another Kennedy named for old Honey Fitz, the biggest crook in Boston history. How 'bout that?"

"The poor little thing's in a respirator," Miss Rankin said.

"Really?" said Gordon's mother, who never read the papers. "Why is that?"

"Premature," Miss Rankin said. "Six pounds three ounces. They say preemies are subject to, you know, breathing problems."

"Well!" Miss Alderhoff said. "It wasn't just *that*. They had to take it with a cesarean."

"Another Caesar in the Kennedy family," brother Peter said in triumph.

Beverly shook her forefinger sidewise at Peter. "Doesn't follow," she said, sounding testy. "The operation wasn't named for Caesar. Caesar was given the name that the operation already had, *sectio caesaria*, because he was born that way. That's the story that . . . P-Pliny the Elder tells, anyway."

Peter looked as though he'd been slapped. Gordon suddenly felt breathless, as if he had been jogging a little too fast.

"Actually," Beverly good-humoredly went on, "that doesn't make too much sense, because in those days they used cesareans only to save the baby when the mother died in ch-childbirth, and we know that Caesar's mother lived for more than f-fifty years after he was born. The f-first recorded cesarean on a living woman was about f-fifteen hundred. It was done by a Swiss . . . p-pig-gelder on his own wife."

The whole table was in silence. Only Uncle Bert, still wearing his orange hat, went on chewing. Gordon got up the courage to look at his mother, and he saw that she was beaming at Beverly. She had a look of amazement and delight on her face. "Mr. Cannahan," she said, "give Beverly a little more wine." Gordon, vibrating with pleasure, saw that the day was going to be a total success after all. The one thing he had been nervous about was Bev's unpredictable spurts of contrariness. He had been afraid of an inadvertent collision of some sort. Bev didn't mean anything by these little bumpy moments; they were for fun, though sometimes others didn't look at them that way. She had an octopus of a memory, and she knew a great deal (some of what she "knew" wasn't exactly so, but never mind), and it would have been hard to say whether she loved best sparring with brilliant people or straightening stupid people out. It was a secret of the constant peacefulness between her and Gordon that she seemed to consider Gordon neither brilliant nor stupid but just comfortably sensible. At this moment he felt a surge in his appetite. He loved Flo's oyster dish.

Miss Rankin piped up. "I wonder if they're going to have the Kennedy family nurse to take care of the baby," she said. "I imagine she took care of Jack himself and all his siblings when they were little. Think of the continuity of it! Miss Hennessy's her name."

"I doubt if they use the 'Miss,' " Miss Alderhoff said. "They'd just call her by her last name. 'Hennessy, would you change the baby's didies, please?' "

"You better believe no Kennedy would have anything to do

with dirty diapers," Peter said with some spirit, looking right at Bev.

But Beverly seemed to have lost interest in Peter. Gordon saw that she had picked up one of the highly polished silver serving spoons that had not been used and was looking at her reflection on the back of it. What a long balloon face she would have in such a mirror! Yet she apparently saw the mess her hair was in, because she began patting it into place. Gordon thought with pleasure, She wants to leave herself in this house—for Bev had a theory that faces printed themselves on mirrors and stayed there forever. She had given herself to one of his mother's spoons.

Peter apparently didn't like Bev's not paying attention to him, and he said, still looking at her, "He's not President yet, thank God. I should have put that in my prayer."

Gordon rose to this. "A little more time for your fatuous Ike to play golf—right? Or like this week, taking care of shop on a quail shoot on some guy's estate in Georgia?"

"Now, boys," Mrs. Bronson said, "act your age. How many times have we seen this, Amos?" she said, smiling at Mr. Cannahan. "Every time these two grown men come home and sit down at the table, it only takes them half an hour to slip back and be ten and eight years old. Isn't that so?"

Mr. Cannahan obviously wanted to agree with his old friend the hostess, but you could also see that he didn't want to offend Gordon and Peter—not at their mother's table—and especially not the lovely young thing on his left, around whom these family breezes seemed in some mysterious way to be swirling. He held his tongue.

Miss Alderhoff, in tune with all pains and sorrows, both at this table and elsewhere, said, "Mr. Eisenhower shouldn't have gone out shooting in the rain, poor man. He has bursitis, you know."

Gordon could see his mother sagging somewhat in her chair.

This, he knew, meant that she was groping with her foot under the table for the bulge of the bell button under the rug down there. Then he must have found it; he heard the buzzer in the kitchen, and Flo burst in. "We'll need another bottle of red wine up here, Flo," his mother said. "How's the supply down at that end, Beth?"

"We could use another bottle," Aunt Beth said.

"White or red, Beth?"

"It's all the same to *me*," Aunt Beth said. She laughed her tinkling laugh.

"I think red here, too, Mother," Gordon said.

"Two red," Flo said, giving the swinging door a little whack with the flat of her hand as she left the room.

"You were playing Sibelius before," Beverly said to Gordon's mother. "Do you specially like his music?"

"Oh, yes. Do you know 'The Swan of Tuonela'?"

"Then you must also like Brahms," Beverly said. "And probably Rachmaninoff. I was th-thinking, why is it that really good pianists and conductors seem to live forever? When I was a little girl, my mother took me to hear Rachmaninoff, he was an old, old man, playing two of his concertos with the Philharmonic. Two concertos in one evening. I think I fell asleep, but I've never forgotten—that old man's f-frightening . . . p-power."

"Ah, Beverly," Gordon's mother said, her face winy and soft, "I can't wait to be really old. That regime! You wake up at five-thirty or so, and they give you a cup of hot milk. You snooze a bit until breakfast. Then you sit for a while under the dogwood tree and doze off. Later, you walk over to look at the strawberries, and then you go back to your chair and they bring you some hot consommé, but you're bored with consommé, so you don't take it, you just sit there: the spots of sun filtering through the tiny white saucers of the dogwood blossoms are so dazzling. Good heavens, you must have dropped off, it's lunchtime! After lunch you lie down on the sofa with a knitted throw over you. Then you get up and play some solitaire. A bath. A highball. Supper. You fall asleep listening to the radio—only that's not your night-sleep—you'll need a toddy to insure your night-sleep. And then they put you to bed, and they actually tuck you in like a child. Think of it!"

Gordon felt a rush of gratitude. Beverly was so fine. Her face, like his mother's, was rosy and melted and a tiny bit swollen by the warmed blood of friendliness. Her scarf had slid down off to the left, and he stared at the curve of her bare pink neck down onto her pale bare shoulder. Suddenly, putting his fork down, he was overcome by a wish that he could get up and go around there and take Bev by the hand, and lead her upstairs to his old room, and receive her in his boyhood bed, and celebrate with her what there was to be most thankful for on this earth.

But Miss Rankin, who was perhaps not looking forward quite so eagerly as Gordon's mother to being "really old," broke his spell. She said in a cranky voice, "Did anyone see David Susskind interviewing Khrushchev in New York the other night?"

"Sure did," Uncle Solbert said, his orange hat askew. "He gave the old bugger what for, didn't he?"

"Did you notice," Miss Alderhoff said, "that Khrushchev drank mineral water instead of coffee during the program? He must have indigestion."

Little Freddie spoke up for the first time. "Susskind sucks," he said.

"I hope the big K does have a bad stomach," Peter said, speaking again straight to Bev. "God damn peasant."

"That's just it, Peter!" Beverly said. "Every clever Russian wants you to *think* he's a peasant. Did you ever read Gorky's reminiscence of . . . T-Tolstoy?" Gordon smiled at the thought of Peter reading even the morning paper. "Gorky read a story of his out loud to Tolstoy, and Tolstoy said he'd got his p-peasants all wrong. The old man said a Russian peasant will come up to you and talk in a silly and incoherent way. He does this on . . . p-purpose, so you'll think he's . . . st-stupid. He knows that people are open and direct with stupid people, and that's just what he wants, because you blurt out everything, you show all your c-cards, and right away he knows your . . . w-weaknesses."

"I think Beverly has a point there, Peter," Gordon's mother said, tapping Peter on the shoulder.

Peter colored violently. He started to say something, but Beverly had turned to Mr. Cannahan, who had finished his mashed bananas, and she was saying, "I like people with weak stomachs. It means that they . . . th-think about things. Maybe they think too m-much sometimes. But at least they think." As she said that last sentence she swerved her gaze back toward Peter.

Gordon saw that his mother was charmed by Beverly's kindness to Mr. Cannahan, and Mr. Cannahan looked as if he might faint from pleasure. But Peter was still very red, and as he chewed, his lower jaw seemed to push out like a bulldozer blade. Gordon knew he must break in somehow, to change the drift of things.

He urgently pinged the back of his knife against his wineglass and then raised the glass and said, "Here's to the two women I love most in this world."

He knew on the instant that he had made a terrible mistake. He saw his mother, faced with the appalling idea of equivalence, suddenly looking at him as if she had no idea who he was. Bev, stricken pale, reached for her wineglass, presumably to raise it to his mother, or perhaps, Gordon thought in sudden panic, to throw it down the whole length of the table at him, but instead she clumsily knocked it over, and a flood of red, like guilty blood, soaked into one of the priceless lace doilies.

A dead silence followed, a pause in which a creaking of dry timbers could be heard, as if the whole house around them were heaving a deep sigh. Then came such a rush of exclamations that Gordon had a sensation of watching a speeded-up footage of film.

Peter cried out, "Ha!"

"Salt! Salt!" Aunt Beth shouted. "Put a lot of salt on it. I tell you, it's the only way to prevent a stain."

Beverly said, all too distinctly, "Sh-shit!" and then quickly added, "I'm s-so s-sorry, Mrs. Bronson."

"Jesus Christ," Peter said.

Uncle Solbert, absurd in his orange paper hat, said in a shocked voice, "Peter!"

Gordon's mother said to Peter, "Watch your tongue, Son. Have you forgotten what day this is?"—as if she herself had forgotten what day it actually was.

Old Miss Alderhoff pushed her chair back and stood up. "Well!" she said, "*I* am going to get a box of salt," and she marched around the table to the kitchen door.

Peter's wife, Molly, at Gordon's left, chose this moment to shout, "Mother Bronson, you've *always* favored Gordon over Petie. *Always.* You're not fair!"

Gordon's mother snapped out, "You stay out of this, Molly."

Little Caroline stood up, knocked her chair over backward, and ran sobbing into the living room. Awful Freddie's eyes were popping out with his first signs of pleasure all day. Miss Alderhoff appeared, with Flo right behind her holding high a blue cylindrical box as if it were the Statue of Liberty's torch, and they strode around the table in tandem. "Where is it? Where is it?" Flo kept asking. Uncle Solbert pointed; Flo leaned over his shoulder and poured a heap of salt on Beverly Zimmer's taint.

Gordon's first thought, scanning his mother's face for what might happen next, was that she suddenly looked a hundred. It was as if she'd got, all at once, her wish to be "really old." The caverns under her eyes had gone dark, her cheeks were bloodless, and the left side of her mouth sagged as if she'd had a stroke. He thought, Oh, God, I've ruined her Thanksgiving. And then, suddenly, with a forkful of maple-flavored turnip on his tongue and with his eyes abruptly peeled to truths for which there was no way of giving thanks, he saw the appalling emptiness, the bleakness, of his mother's life. Here she sat in a dark house with her best friends: two gossipy old maids and a man whose stomach burned year after year with the acidity of his enigmatic needs—three companions of her days and nights in empty prattle during endless bridge games. On top of that, she'd had to cope with her alcoholic brother Solbert and alcoholic sister-in-law Beth, who lived nearby. And then her raging son Peter; and his Molly, with a voice like the one you heard as a child on a tin-can telephone with a string stretched to the speaker's can; and their rotten children, her only grandchildren, affording her, too sadly, a hollow pride in her legacy. And then: what of the other son, at that moment swallowing turnip—what of him?

Gordon's mother turned to Beverly and asked in a kindly voice, "What do you like about my son?"

Gordon wondered what sort of trap his mother was setting.

"G-Gordon? Gordon?" Beverly asked twice, perhaps to stall for time. "What I like about G-Gordon is that he doesn't . . . sm-smoke cigars."

Mrs. Bronson laughed. "Good for you!" she said with generous admiration, as if Beverly had managed to drive a passing shot over the net that was stretched between them.

"Do you have any idea why he likes you?"

It was Beverly's turn to laugh. "He likes my being . . . di-di-di-disorderly. In my . . . th-thinking. You see, your son is very neat—very careful which dr-drawers he p-puts things in."

Gordon saw that the color was coming back into his mother's face. By God, she was a strong one, she had recovered, she was enjoying herself. He was tempted to ask his mother what it was in Beverly that *she* was beginning to like, but he was afraid to.

"How 'bout *your* drawers?" Peter said to Beverly. "Is he, like you say, c-careful?"

Little Freddie snickered.

"Shut *up*, Peter!" Uncle Solbert shouted.

"My heavens," Mr. Cannahan said.

"Molly," Gordon's mother said, projecting a hushed voice the length of the table, "sometimes your husband can be very annoying. But I'm sure you know that of your own knowledge." She turned back to Beverly and said, "Tell me more about my Gordon."

"Well," Bev said, "he's sort of muh-muh . . . m-*my* Gordon right now."

"Ah," Mrs. Bronson said. "You stake a claim. Do you believe his intentions are honorable, as they used to say?"

"Better ask him," Beverly said without a trace of a stammer.

"Gordon," his mother said, "serve some more turkey to whoever wants it, please."

Gordon felt a stab of anger. Having said that he and Peter reverted to being eight and ten years old at her table, his mother was now, for her purposes, treating him like a child. Staking *her* claim, he guessed. Careful to control his voice, he said, "Beverly and I are going to be married."

Uncle Solbert tore his paper hat off and waved it in circles over his head and shouted, "Hurray!"

"Congratulations," Mr. Cannahan said to Beverly, looking heartbroken.

"My God," Peter said.

"And you chose to tell me this at Thanksgiving dinner?" Gordon's mother said.

"I thought you'd be happy for me, Mother."

"Oh, but I am," she said, her voice trembling. "You have picked a winner. You've shown very good sense, Son." She turned to Beverly and said, her eyes brimming, "I have liked you, Miss Zimmer, from the moment you walked in the front door. My Gordon, if you will permit me to call him that once more, is a very lucky boy."

After a long pause Beverly said, "Your p-peach ch-chutney is the b-best I ever tasted."

"Thank you, my dear." Gordon saw his mother's face relax into a terrible smile of surrender, and he felt a rush of contrition and pity. She was amazing. She had caught her balance. "Marriage," she was saying to Bev, "isn't an easy estate. You'd better have a little chat with Molly down there about it. I was fairly lucky myself, but it wasn't easy, you know. My husband was an indecisive man, and—"

But Miss Alderhoff had raised her glass, and was calling out in a shrill voice, "Let's drink to the engagement. To Gordon and Miss Zimmer!"

"Yes! Yes!" cried Miss Rankin. "To the engagement!"

Uncle Solbert and Aunt Beth both cheered, but others at the table were quiet as they lifted their glasses and drank. Peter hesitated.

"Drink up, darling," Gordon's mother said to Peter. She seemed to be herself again. She caressed his arm. "Wish your brother luck, darling."

"Here's mud in your eye," Peter said to Gordon, before he gulped at his glass. He did not look at Beverly.

Why Were You Sent Out Here?

With abrupt acceleration, the heavy revolving front door of the Wagons-Lits Hotel started to swing around. After the door flaps had thudded twice, Colonel Potter Watson emerged on the outer side. He was about thirty-five years old, florid and strong-looking. He had on his lapels the brass vial and flame of Chemical Warfare, and he displayed, above his left breast pocket, only one overseas ribbon—a brand-new Asian Theater stripe. When he had stepped clear, the door slowed down a lot and let out Colonel William de Angelis, who wore the insignia of an infantryman and several decorations from the First World War. The second officer's face, that of a man about sixty, was a pattern of meaningless lines on contours that had apparently been interesting once, like an action map in a rear-echelon headquarters after the fighting is over. Everything about the older man looked slightly dilapidated, except for a beautiful, flexible, braided swagger stick tucked under his left arm.

Colonel Watson stepped out to the front of the marble platform of the entranceway and greeted the heavy Chinese doorman by name: "Good morning, Sung."

The doorman tipped his visored khaki hat and said, "Good morning, master," and bowed slightly.

The older colonel, coming along behind, said dully, "Good day."

"Good morning, sir," Sung replied, and did not bow to the older man. He told the officers that the eight-o'clock shuttle bus to Peking Union Medical College, their headquarters, had just left.

Colonel Watson, the younger officer, said, "Nice spring morning like this, why don't we take a ricksha?" Colonel de Angelis acquiesced. Sung lifted a fat hand as a signal to the coolies lounging on the footboards of a row of fancy Legation Quarter rickshas across the street. Several grabbed up the shafts of their vehicles and ran, pulling the rickshas, across to the entranceway and shouted competitively for the Americans' favor. Colonel Watson, recognizing a puller he had engaged once before, said, "I'll take Number Thirty-four here." Colonel de Angelis, who did not know one coolie from another, accepted the most insistent puller. This man had run up the steps and was actually trying to push the elderly colonel toward his own ricksha. "All right," Colonel de Angelis said, "take your hands off me."

Instead of giving instructions in English to Sung for translation, Colonel Watson spoke directly to his coolie in fairly well pronounced Chinese: "To Executive Headquarters. How are you today?"

The coolie mumbled a reply and pulled out ahead. The older colonel's puller followed.

Colonel Watson turned and said over his shoulder to his companion in the other ricksha, "No dust today. Look at that sky."

The two rickshas turned in to Legation Street. Along the sidewalks, the horse chestnuts and acacias, whose leaves had suddenly fanned out from buds after a rain the week before, were still and fragrant. Policemen in black uniforms argued noisily in front of a large building on the left, which they were apparently appropriating as a station; their hubbub seemed to be all about how to unload some furniture they were moving. A couple of Chinese college girls rode up the street on bicycles, careless of the way their slit dresses exposed their thighs; Colonel Watson watched them, but the older man did not. He was looking, as he had been bid to do, at the sky. How sharply the roof tiles of the buildings they passed were edged against the blue! And what blue! Pure, a color one could see only over Peking, with the sheen of old porcelain, he thought. He saw Colonel Watson turn again and heard him shout cheerfully, "Spring moves along a lot faster here than it does in Hartford!"

Colonel de Angelis found the younger man's exuberance annoying. He realized all at once that he had nothing specific and absolute with which to compare the North China weather, for he had nothing to remember as home—just the series of camps that a regular Army man passes through. Was there ever spring at Fort Bragg or Camp Mills or Fort Sam Houston? How fast did all those seasons move along? Colonel Watson's remarks, whether he intended them to be or not, were irritating. He remembered, in sudden focus—as, for some reason, he had quite a few times in recent days while he had been rooming with Colonel Watson—several scenes at Fort Sam Houston: a parade there, the barbershop on the post, his desk at C Company headquarters.

As the rickshas swung into Rue Marco Polo and passed a couple of curio shops, Colonel Watson leaned around again and called out, "Don't get sucked into those places. Terrible gyp joints. Have you been down to Embroidery Street?"

"No."

"I'll take you down there someday. Chinese city. Same stuff as up here, only you can bargain. I'll take you down."

Colonel de Angelis decided at once that he did not want to go to Embroidery Street with Colonel Watson, who surely would bully the merchants and boast later of his triumphs. Colonel de Angelis was rather surprised at the vehemence of his feeling about the younger officer. Ever since they had been put in the same room at the hotel, he had been annoyed by little things Watson did—his long throat-clearing sessions in the bathroom in the mornings, his frequent and positive contradictions of what people said, his excellent appetite, his constant good spirits, his knowing everything and wanting to be so helpful—but Colonel de Angelis had not realized so clearly before how much he really disliked his roommate. Colonel de Angelis thought again of Fort Sam Houston; something about that place had been trying to crowd into his memory ever since he had spent his first day with Watson. Maybe, he decided, it was because he had been about Watson's age when he was there. That was in 1921 and 1922; twenty-four and -five years ago. Yes, he thought, that must be it.

Colonel Watson had turned around again. "I got a honey of a shantung table set down there," he said, "a breakfast set, I think you call it. Only seven bucks. I knocked 'em down from twelve." Then Watson snapped his fingers at Colonel de Angelis's ricksha puller and said to him in English, "Say, boy, hubba-hubba a bit. Come alongside here." He beckoned and flagged the coolie up. "The colonel and I want to talk to each other. That's better."

The rickshas ran parallel. "Seems funny," Watson said, "the way they sent so many of us over here at once—colonels and lieutenant colonels. Like it, so far?"

"Well," Colonel de Angelis said, "the food in the hotel is certainly punk. If they offer me another of those cold rice pancakes for breakfast—"

"I don't know," Colonel Watson said, as he always did in preface to a disagreement. "They have a darn good steak in the grill. I don't think the food is so bad." He paused, then said, "How did they happen to send you out here? Did you ever hear?"

Colonel de Angelis wondered: Why did they send a hundred colonels and lieutenant colonels over to North China in one batch? Couldn't they have used more majors and captains in the teams to monitor the truce between the Gissimo and the Commies? And how did they happen to choose one man or another from the tremendous replacement pool? How did they happen to pick so many men who had been passed over for promotion, and so many who had already been bumped back from brigadier? Why *did* they send me over here? The older colonel shrugged. "You know the Army," he said.

"I put in for this duty," Watson said. "The way I figured was, with the war over and me not getting overseas while it was on, China seemed like the best possible chance for advancement—for a younger man, that is," he added.

Colonel de Angelis thought again of Fort Sam. What was it he was trying to recall? At Fort Sam Houston he had been a captain. Those were dismal barracks. He had had the fourth bunk from the end on the right side in G. His sergeant major—what was his name? Benny something-or-other—that was great the time Benny pretended to trip and butted into Rassmussen. What a pathetic old character Captain Rassmussen was!

A silver C-54 roared low over the city and for a moment it seemed to be framed, from where the colonels rode, within the pailou, the high, skeletal ceremonial gate near the top of Rue Marco Polo. "Look at that!" Colonel Watson shouted, and at once he launched into what was certain, if past recitals meant anything, to be a long account of his uneventful flight across the Pacific. Colonel de Angelis only half listened. The rasping, effusive voice went on and on: ". . . hit the runway right on the nose, and we hadn't been out of the overcast since Kwajalein . . ."; the story touched on all the commonplaces. Colonel de Angelis tried to distract himself by looking at the market, already crowded and obstreperous, spread out on the old glacis of the Legation Quarter, to their right as they rode—at the too colorful Japanese obis hung like wash on a line; booths where cloth shoes, old bottles, peanuts, suitcases, sweet potatoes, Chinese fiddles were for sale; men hawking, arguing in shouts, and talking loudly simply to be heard; and, at some distance on the curb, a bicycle-tire repairer waiting patiently a few yards beyond an area of broken glass he had scattered in the street. Colonel de Angelis remembered that he had had a bicycle at Fort Sam Houston. Fort Sam after the first war hadn't seemed such a bad place; there was not much to do except avoid mistakes. On the whole, looking back, it was pretty good duty. A captaincy is a satisfying rank, when you're young. It couldn't have been so much fun for Captain Rassmussen, at his age. (". . . I never saw so many wrecked ships," Colonel Watson was saying, "as we did going in over Buckner Bay. My God, that must have been some typhoon . . .") Colonel de Angelis, called back by the younger man's voice when it seemed all at once to get louder, wondered what it was he so disliked about Colonel Watson. The other newcomers seemed to like him all right; they considered him cheerful, a good drinker, marvelous at liars' dice, skillful at bargaining with the Chinks—a great fellow, they said. One man had even congratulated de Angelis on the luck of his draw for roommate. Anyone could room with Watson who wanted to. Perhaps, Colonel de Angelis thought, he could speak to the Chinese WASC representative at the hotel that afternoon and get himself shifted to a single room. Let's see, he thought, get a haircut, go over to the PX for nail scissors—what was the other thing he had to do in the afternoon? (". . . absolutely clear over Shanghai . . .") What *was* it Watson brought to his mind—or to the very edge of his mind? Was it, he wondered for a moment, something about Captain Rassmussen?

On the way into Morrison Street, Watson directed the ricksha coolies, in Chinese, to turn in toward Executive Headquarters at the third hutung, rather than the second, so that
they could go in the side entrance. "You taking up Chinese?"
he asked Colonel de Angelis. "Or," he went on in an affec-
tionately teasing tone, "are you one of these old dogs that
refuse to learn new tricks? Helps a lot, I can tell you. I got a
start on it back in the States. You see, I got wind of this
assignment—" He paused, as if waiting to be told that he
would always land on *his* feet, and then went on, as if taking
the compliment for granted, "It doesn't hurt to keep some
wires out. So when I heard about this, I lined myself up to
have a couple of months in the language school up at New
Haven. I still work on it pretty hard. It makes a difference,
specially on bargaining. These merchants dope it out that they
can't fool around; anybody that speaks even a few words must
be an old China hand, that's the way they figure it. You meet
a different type of people, too, with the language. You take
down in Shanghai, while we were waiting to be shipped up
here, I darn near got myself lined up with a sleeping dictionary.
She was a honey. Belonged to a second lieutenant who got
shipped home."

The rickshas turned off Morrison Street into the third alley
on the right. The older man looked at the headquarters compound, which now came into sight at the dead end ahead—
the massive, handsome, pseudo-Oriental buildings that had
once comprised a hospital and medical school, endowed by the
Rockefellers, he had heard; now a house divided three ways
—two kinds of Chinese and some Americans, all ostensibly
trying to bring an end to civil war. What could he do there?
He knew nothing about China. Every day he grew more con-
fused as he watched the opposing Chinese and the Americans
addressing one another with elaborate but artificial gestures,
like those of marionettes, as if they were trying by sheer energy

to make convincing the things they were saying—things that nobody could possibly believe. He had been in Peking two weeks, and still there had been no decision about whether he would be in the operations section here in Peking or would be sent out with a field team. He was somehow afraid of the buildings, with the kind of vague fear he would have felt if the compound were still a hospital, with ether heavy in the corridors.

Colonel Watson, who had also been looking at the buildings, turned and asked, "No, really, aside from the food, do you think you're going to like it here?"

Like it? Like it? "I guess it'll be all right."

And then, unmistakably, in the sound of that "Like it?" he recognized the one whom Colonel Watson reminded him of: it was himself.

The Crescent, though by no means the finest speakeasy in San Antonio in 1921, nor that with the safest liquor, seemed to attract more soldiers and officers than any other. Its mirrors, cheap smoked-wood wainscoting, and brass chandeliers were like those of an old saloon; the place was ironically decorated, Colonel de Angelis remembered, with cartoons of John Barleycorn, photographs of Volstead and Miss Frances Willard and a convention of Band of Hope children, framed clippings of Prohibitionist news, and a cross-stitched motto: "The voters do not have the courage to vote as they drink—Dr. N. M. Butler."

Colonel de Angelis remembered that he and Captain Rassmussen had sat that night—a winter night, late in 1921, it must have been—at a table against the wall opposite the bar. The place was crowded with all sorts: fairly well dressed couples, workmen in denim, girls looking for pickups. Captain de Angelis's uniform was crisp and his buttons bright. Captain

Rassmussen seemed very tired. He was nearly sixty and would never be anything but a captain. He had blond hair with some gray in it, and a ruddy, finely wrinkled face. He had been at Fort Sam Houston only about a month, and de Angelis had asked him, a few days before, to take a seventy-two with him to San Antonio.

When he had invited Rassmussen, de Angelis had believed he did it because he liked the older man, who had been cheerful enough around the post, and full of stories of the old-time Army; on the way into San Antonio, he had decided it had been because he pitied Rassmussen; and after a few hours in the town, when he had found that the older man had no appetite for food, hadn't the faintest desire to work up a date with a girl, wanted only two drinks, was satisfied with a captaincy, did not dislike his superiors, laughed about everything but never as if he meant it, wanted nothing, had nothing, was nothing—then de Angelis realized that he resented Rassmussen. He began to tease him. At first he was fairly subtle, and stuck so close to the truth, alternately praising and criticizing the elderly captain, that Rassmussen could not, at first, be anything but gratified, if slightly puzzled, by his young friend's interest in him.

Later, however, when de Angelis found that his anger at the older man only grew with his own elation, he began to be comparatively obvious. He talked about the Army's retirement and pension systems. He remarked that he had noticed how exhausted Rassmussen had looked out on parade a couple of days before. And he asked over and over whether Rassmussen liked being a captain at his age. Eventually this had become a half-drunken refrain: "Do you like it? Do you like it?" At last the older officer said, without particular anger, but looking quite defeated, "Say, I believe you're being darned unkind." De Angelis apologized and protested—quite convincingly, he felt—that he hadn't meant a thing by his remarks.

. . .

The rickshas pulled up at the side gate of the headquarters compound. Colonel Watson asked in Chinese how much his coolie wanted, and after several sentences of conversation, in which mock outrage was displayed on both sides, he gave the coolie some bills and turned away laughing.

"How much do you give these jokers?" Colonel de Angelis asked.

"Let him have five hundred," Watson said. "It's too much, but he'll give you a better ride next time."

Colonel de Angelis handed his puller some bills. At once the coolie began protesting in noisy Chinese. "What's he saying?" the older colonel asked Watson.

"Just the usual stink. Come on."

Colonel de Angelis stepped over the shafts and started toward the entranceway. The coolie followed with hands outstretched, sneering at the bills he held, talking louder and louder, higher and higher, and—it seemed to Colonel de Angelis—more and more abusively. The older colonel turned and said with as much authority and contempt as he could convey in a language that would not be understood, "That's enough. Now hang up." He wheeled and walked on. But the coolie only shouted more, and he ran and caught up with the colonel and put a dirty hand on the officer's sleeve and then grabbed the sleeve and waved the bills in front of the American's face.

"Come on!" Colonel Watson shouted. He was about ten paces ahead.

The coolie tugged hard at Colonel de Angelis's sleeve. The elderly colonel turned abruptly and, reaching across with his right hand, pulled out his swagger stick and aimed and flashed it backhand.

Colonel de Angelis glanced around and saw that Watson

had started walking springily—perhaps tactfully; had he seen?—up the steps into the entrance court. Colonel de Angelis looked out to see if there had been any American officers coming along the street; there had not. The coolie stood with his right hand partly hiding the red stripe the swagger stick had printed on his cheek, his left hand still stretched out waving the paper money; he was silent now.

With a slow, awkward, exaggerated movement, like that of a drunken man, Colonel de Angelis groped in his breast pocket for his wallet, took it out, opened it, got out a bill, and offered it to the coolie, who took it and turned away without speaking. Colonel de Angelis stepped rather erratically toward the entrance. The two Chinese sentries standing at the gate saluted him with mechanical eagerness. He transferred the swagger stick from his right hand back under his left arm, and returned their greeting. As the old colonel started up the steps, he saw that the younger man was already indoors. There didn't seem to be any faces in the windows around the wide entrance court.

Requiescat

The moment I hated most at Thurston's came toward the end of Winston Fief's tribute. I had tried to talk Margot out of having the service at Thurston's at all. Moose Bradford didn't belong in one of those fashionable horror shows at James W. Thurston's "Memorial Chapel," which are treated in the next day's *Times* like Met openings or muscular-dystrophy balls at the Waldorf. Moose had given up on New York. He despised that crowd. I put it to Margot that services at Thurston's were like big parties publishers give for hot authors at Four Seasons—big winners and burnt-out cases scouting each other, new outfits on display, envy on the loose, nothing to do with a figure like Moose. Who would get the best pews? God, look at that hat of Cynthia's, has St.-Laurent gone bonkers? That would be the level of the text. But Margot is Margot.

The room was Thurston's largest. The design of the pews, and indeed the mode of the place as a whole, was right enough for Moose—decorous, understated, New Englandish, more or less Congregational, almost in the spirit of the simple church he loved so much on Greenfield Hill. But you could count on Margot to have the last word. Her final affront to Moose was to smother him, where he lay in his brass-handled box—

Margot had told me the casket was Thurston's four-thousand-dollar number—in gladioluses. Moose hated them. I remember once his calling them the Pekingese dogs of the gardening world. He said they literally nauseated him, and I believed him; it was part of Moose's makeup to have powerful somatic reactions to flowers, as he did to many other things—pets, colors, good and bad news, and the sight of a strange woman's bare shoulder. He spent half his life having goose pimples.

As I entered, about fifteen minutes early, I could see that the room was going to be packed to overflowing—a flock of fickle ego-trippers who had forgotten how cruelly they'd snubbed Moose back in the fifties, now suddenly titillated by his horrible death, all turning up: celebrities, jet-setters, writers, politicians, musicians, business types, and ex-radicals wearing three-piece custom-made suits. A queer gazpacho. Having suffered my own loss so recently, I was feeling low anyway, and the sight of these people who thought this the best ticket in town that morning took me down a further notch.

Margot had given Thurston's ushers a list, and they put me in the second pew on the left, right behind three of Moose's four wives, all in a row. Maria, poor thing, was absent in the death of her own choosing, but the three survivors were there, chatting away like catbirds, Margot impeccable as hostess to those other two bitches, as she refers to them. I felt hot. This was not good enough for Moose; with all his weaknesses, Moose was a serious man.

Margot had Grischa Wallenstein play the viola for a while, a stately Bach chaconne—just right to choose the deep-toned instrument that is usually subordinated, almost too big to tuck under the chin, and Grischa, on slight acquaintance, seemed to have understood Moose, because he made Bach sound somehow akin to Hawthorne and Melville and Dickinson. That would have been enough, just that music, with its strange controlled leaps from string to string, from constraint to constraint, but also from heartbeat to wild heartbeat.

But then came the three so-called tributes, each worse than I could have feared: Eliot Fanton, sounding as if he were arguing a somehow distasteful civil-rights case before the Supreme Court; Philip Sieveringhaus, who hardly knew Moose at all but was "in" enough to suit Margot, reading a long boozy poem he'd probably torn off the night before, really an abstract thanatopsis rather than a remembrance of this dead man; and Winston Fief—I'll come to him. In all three performances I was reminded of the way Hazel, Moose's first wife, used to pay her husband fulsome and obviously insincere compliments—keeping him on a tight leash.

All three touched on Moose's courage, but as if it were beyond his command, demonic; on his having gone to prison for his beliefs, though under the surface admiration there were whiffs of a sick awe, as if there had been something in Moose really criminal, something that belonged in prison; on his "vitality," his "magnetic energy," which everyone understood with a little mental snicker to mean his voracious pursuit of the skirt; and—archly—on the "senseless violence" of his death. All three, even the poet, used that very phrase. To me, the violence had made all too much sense. It was the native-as-apple-pie goal toward which Moose had been steering all his turbulent life long, the failed Puritan's final collision with the earthy reality he had always yearned for. I felt the same anger at those three men as I did at whoever had killed Moose in the first place.

Win Fief was all dressed in leather—open-necked shirt, jacket, and flaring trousers, enough cowhide against the skin to make a Buddhist pass out; at his neck a discrete little French sailor's scarf; Birkenstock sandals; hairstyle like Boy George's. He seemed to have had a dream of youth. About ten years younger than Moose and I—no youth he. I never could figure out what Moose saw in him, but he really liked Win. Win talked as much about himself, in his "tribute," as he did about Moose: "When I first met our friend, I had just finished the preliminary designs for the Cullinan building. . . ." But what really set me on edge was a complicated idea Win tried to develop about "origins and style," for in putting this passage together Win's pretensions had got the best of him, and he missed Moose by a mile. For a gross example: "His was a world fundamentally Emersonian, Thoreauvian, Jamesian." Moose loathed Emerson, thought Thoreau self-righteous, admired James but felt light-years distant from his fastidiousness. Grischa with his big deep fiddle had understood: Moose came from that other New England, the New England of the wild heartbeat. The culmination of this passage of Win's was the sentence that almost made me get up and walk out.

"He was your decent sort of WASP—no sting."

An architect should never be entrusted with words. A shallow conceit like that one was bad enough in itself, but beyond that it was a knowing falsehood. Moose was all sting. Winston Fief knew him. It had never occurred to me before to wonder whether Win was Jewish. I felt in the line a hint of that reciprocal face of anti-Semitism, the Jew's despising of the goy. That hostility, though, is usually relieved by, discharged through, wit, and Win's line was not only unwitty, it was witless. But it did have a lot of veiled malice in it, condescension, and even hatred. All from Moose's "friend." This was really why I had tried to argue Margot out of the affair at Thurston's, and why I had refused to speak myself. A stylish funeral service of that sort can't help giving license to subtle encodings of anger, and some not so subtle, and I knew that Moose alive had planted a great deal of that feeling, which dead he would harvest. Anyone as big as he was, literally and figuratively, comes in for his share of envy, resentment, sexual jealousy, and, above all, skepticism—especially where there has been a larger-than-life sense of honor in the makeup. Those negatives were richly embedded in the praise of the so-called tributes. All you had to do was listen with care.

It was worse outside on the bright sidewalk afterward. People lingered. It was a dazzling May noontime, and the scene sparkled like a bottle of mixed hard candies in a sunny window. The maple trees on the cross street, which would be so drab in full leaf in a few weeks, were dressed now in their new lime leaves, shuffling wafer-thin slices of light in the gentle breeze. The gold-on-black lettering of the Thurston's legend running around above the first floor of the building was circumspectly consoling. Dark-suited attendants with pale averted faces, seeming to share some monstrous secret about the deceased, were carrying armfuls of gladioluses of all colors out the side entrance and were banking them in a sunlight-pricked black Cadillac pickup parked in front of the so far empty hearse. The jerky movements of the women in their soft-colored clothes—who wants to look dreary at a funeral?—and their turning, searching glances suggested an irritable restlessness in the letdown of knowing that Moose's enormous sensuality, of which they had all been aware, even from great distances, was quelled now. I saw Cynthia Bigwood's gaze land like a perching bird on Fay Callender's pale green cashmere outfit, which must have been a Donna Karan. Fay Callender stared at the halter—Givenchy?—that made the most of Barclay Delavanty's creamy neck. Round and round the eyes kept flying, as if looking for a promise that time would break its rules now and stand still.

People were embarrassed to see me. I was in my rage. My wife Deborah was dead and buried. My best friend Moose was dead but not buried. I had to hang around, waiting for the motorcade that would carry him out to the country, to the shady plot Margot and I had chosen in Weston. When these people saw me looming, they would break off whatever they were chatting about and say, "Beautiful service," or, "Wasn't Win good?" or, "Dear Hugh, what a charmer old Moosey was."

The ride out to Weston seemed to me to take a month. The three wives rode in the first car, behind the pickup banked with glads. Did those three talk about Moose all the way? What might they have been saying to each other? I was stuck in the second limo, on a jump seat, of course. With me were Grischa Wallenstein, his pale girl Wanda Somethingski, Phil Sieveringhaus, and Phil's wife, the actress Pamela Brighton. When we got in, the great poet shoved his way into the back seat between the two women, and poor Grischa got the other jump seat, while behind him the poet applied his usual feelies to pale Wanda, who kept exclaiming in an East European accent. We went by way of the Merritt. The many dogwoods were stretching out their pretty paper hands to the sun. Sieveringhaus kept asking the limo driver to pull out of line and go someplace to a bar, but the man pretended not to hear.

The graveside ceremony included some fine old language from *The Book of Common Prayer* of the sort Moose liked, and then they put him down, and we heard the thud of the first shovelful of dirt. Afterward there was a kind of cocktail party at Margot and Moose's house—not a word about Moose that I could hear. I was driven back to town alone in one of the limousines.

And yes, the next morning I found the *Times* had had Emily Friller, the social reporter with the heavy ironic touch, cover the service, and she handled it—quite correctly—as a sign of the astonishing change in the culture since the early fifties.

I called Margot. "I hope you're satisfied," I said.

"It was beautiful," she said. "Artur came. Did you see that Lenny was there? I was so happy."

"Happy? That was a funeral. Remember? Moose died?"

"I was happy for him."

I half expected Margot to say that I had a few things to learn, that a memorial service isn't to remember the dead, it's to be glad that that person died and not you.

"I have to have a talk with you," I said.

Grief first struck me a hard blow in the chest when I walked into the Weston living room the next evening, and Margot was there in her red chair but Moose was *not* standing in front of the fireplace with one hand up on the mantel near his Old Grand-Dad on the rocks, his weight on one hip-sprung leg, his broad, mobile face working itself around an anecdote neither of us had heard before. In the grip of this vivid notness, I think I saw him in memory as clearly as I ever had in the flesh.

First, the head. It bobbed and tucked with emphases, was lifted for an expectant pause. It was one of the great heads of all time. During the period when Moose was a frequent tenant of the gossip columns, his head was compared with those of John L. Lewis, Judge Learned Hand, Arturo Toscanini, Pablo Picasso, Wendell Willkie. When we think of such men, we speak of the lion, which, besides his huge mane, has a prodigious sack of stones between his hind legs, and indeed there was an open maleness and a hint of profligate raunchiness about all those men. There certainly was about Moose. There is no sensualist like a massive Puritan.

He moved like a big cat. I remember the first time I saw him running down under a pass on Baker Field at Hotchkiss. I was in the bleachers, exiled from sports by a heart murmur. (My flawed ticker out-ticked his.) In those days football players wore pliable leather helmets snug on the skull, and because of his enormous shoulder pads even his great head seemed proportionately small. He ran, made a head fake and a cut, looked back, and took the ball softly in his huge hands. Once

I asked him if he had a sense of dancing as he went downfield for a pass, and he said, "No. It's all in the eyes. You have to narrow your field of vision. It's like looking through a tube. Rufus throws: all I can see is the ball coming into the other end of the tube. I just put my hands around the near end of the tube, and the ball comes into them."

All in the eyes. The shaggy brows—like a wingspread—remained black as his hair grayed. Under them the brown-irised eyes were disconcerting. When they narrowed their focus, they projected, through his "tube," a laserlike beam that could set fire to things; at other times, the look in them went fuzzy, as if the pupils were dissolving, and then the eyes seemed scooped out and blackly hollow, and in the hollow place there was a chill like that in an ancient cistern.

How could a Puritan have such thick lips? Deep parenthetical lines ran down from the flanges of his nose to the sides of his mouth—they always had, even when he was a boy—so his wide and otherwise cheerful face always looked haunted.

His great hands flopped around like flags. They were broad, spatulate, and remarkably dry, as dry as papyrus. His right hand, as you gripped it in greeting, was a shock: limp, dead-fishy, veddy British. Many people, having once shaken hands with him, thought Moose Bradford cold and snooty, a New England snob to the fingertips. What they couldn't know, because he never talked about it, was that three of the flexor muscles on the inside of his right forearm were snipped off clean by a ricocheting hunk of the Zero that kamikazied on the signal bridge of the *Hornet* the day she was sunk—on that mysterious day that cast a shadow over all the rest of his life.

So there he was, or rather wasn't, in front of the fireplace, just as powerful in absence as he had been in the flesh.

"What did you want to talk about, old Hugh?"

Moose had called me "old Hugh" ever since prep school,

and I did not at all like Margot's appropriating that phrase. I said, "I want to write a piece about Moose."

Margot looked as if I'd insulted her; perhaps she thought I'd come—or should have come—to offer condolences, to comfort her in her bereavement, and it was not nice to talk about what I wanted to do.

"How can you write an article about such a close friend? No one will believe you."

"I know, but I'd like to try."

"My Lord, Hughie, have you come to interview me?"

"I want to try to understand some things," I said.

"But, Hugh," she said, not one to waste any time putting on the old brass knuckles, "you wouldn't be able to be fair to him after the way he fooled around with Deborah. Remember? That time? Forget it, Hughie. *Requiescat in pace.*"

Moose lived two lives. He aspired to sainthood and became a sybarite. "I married him," Margot said later that evening, "because he was so decent. He was the first really good man I ever met—the crowd we grew up with, God. Did you ever know any other lawyer who had the kind of integrity he had? Lawyers are trained to take either side, but you knew damn well, Hughie, with every case there was a side Moose wouldn't take no matter how much moola you offered him. But by the time I got him, you know, I found out—too late—the treads were worn off his tires. He'd had it. I don't mean he wasn't sexy, he was all too—but the edge was off the other business, his moral influence, whatever you want to call it. Hazel had the best of him. She had his best years. We talked about that in the limo on the way out to the graveyard. She got him when he came back from the war; he was so gutsy in those years. Poor Maria got him after he came out of prison; she found out that he cheated on her *once*, one time, and you know what happened to her. Then Carol—she was a little too good at cheating herself, huh? Then poor me, what?"

"Poor you," I said. "You kept your hooks in him longer than any of the rest of them."

"I was the only one who knew what he was made of."

"But you two fought all the time."

"He didn't know what he wanted, so he got mad with me when I agreed with him."

I went home that night in a fury at Margot. That was a very strange line of hers: "He didn't know what he wanted." I had always believed that he firmly wanted to do the right thing. Except, of course, where desire was concerned—though there, I suppose, he might have thought that the right thing, every time, is to help yourself. This was the side of him Margot had used to get under my skin, saying, "Remember? That time?"—the time when Moose had "fooled around" with my dear, dead Deborah, who, she seemed to be suggesting, was at that very moment frolicking on the Elysian Fields in the altogether with old stud Moosey. But I did not remember. I never knew that Moose had had a fling with Deb—if he had. "That time?" she'd said. I couldn't ask her, What time? But she must have known I'd spend a lot of effort asking myself that question from then on.

Before I went to bed that night, I thought of my visit to Moose in the federal pen at Attica, and I remembered he was waiting on the other side of the barrier as I sat down, and I was just trying to take in the unfamiliar bulk of him in a gray prison outfit that was much too tight for him—they must not have had anything his size—when he said, first thing, "How's that beautiful Deborah?" Was "that time" before that? After?

I lay awake far into the night trying to chase those questions out of my mind by thinking back to those days, thinking about why Moose had landed in prison in the first place. It was so hard to recapture the crazy hysteria of the first three months of that year. I tried to sort it out. The first thing was the Hiss sentence, must have been January. Then the Klaus Fuchs confession in London. Then McCarthy getting off that first insane speech in Wheeling, West Virginia, "I have here in my hand . . ." And then the case that mattered, of course, to Moose, since he'd represented three of them: the Supreme Court upholding the convictions of the eleven Communist leaders accused under the Smith Act. And then, as the moves came against Moose, barely noticeable in this more sensational context—the Judith Coplon conviction, Julius and Ethel Rosenberg and Harry Gold and David Greenglass arrested for selling the Russians atom-bomb secrets, the *Amerasia* business, and McCarthy back at it with the first charges against Owen Lattimore. The House Un-American Activities Committee picked up on Moose ostensibly because he'd defended three Communists—ignoring the fact that he had always gone on the line for underdogs, no matter what their politics may have been. He got himself in trouble, I'd heard back then, because of his scrupulousness about telling the truth in the hearings he was called in for. He kept saying, "I can't remember precisely." Maybe he was afraid of being caught perjuring himself; he certainly didn't *want* to go to prison. He refused to take the Fifth because, he said, everyone thought that to do that was to confess guilt, and he knew he wasn't guilty of a damn thing. All of Moose's friends believed he'd managed pretty well, but HUAC trumped up a charge of contempt of Congress, and he was sentenced to three months, of which he served one. It wasn't long as prison terms go, but it made him famous, at least in New York, made him one of the heroes or one of the Commies, depending on where you came from. Even the "friends" who said they admired his guts kept away from him for months after that, just to be on the safe side.

As I pondered trying to write about all that, I had, more and more, an uneasy feeling that something was missing. His record was spotless. He'd never had anything to do—except as an attorney—with radicals. If you looked closely, he was conservative: a classic New Englander who would be very doubtful about hasty change of any kind and would certainly register to vote as an Independent. Even in those mad-dog days, with McCarthy and HUAC on the rampage, they weren't going around throwing many straight lawyers like Bradford into prison. I didn't get to sleep until nearly dawn.

As soon as I was dressed the next morning, I went downtown and put in an application, under the Freedom of Information Act, for the Bradford file at the FBI.

The things I care about most are hardest for me to do, and in the weeks after that I kept putting off working on the Moose piece. Then one night at a dinner party I was seated beside Hazel, who according to Margot had "had the best years" of Moose. She's secure in a happy remarriage, these days, to a cheerful, fat, easygoing guy who follows the odd and evidently very profitable occupation of buying and selling diamonds. She was relaxed and generous as she talked about Moose, though I remembered that their divorce—she had brought it—had been messy. And what had made it so unpleasant was that she moved out on him just after he came under fire from HUAC, so that the gossips kept saying she'd found out something nasty about his political past.

"The lovely thing about Moose," she said now, "was that he seemed forever to be trying to figure out how to be an honorable person. It's not so easy, Hughie. He'd charge off in one direction and then another—and then there'd be these little selfishnesses. Self-serving lies. Or anyway inconsistencies. Did you ever play tennis with him?"

"I have a funny heart."

"Of course you do, I'm sorry. It was always 'Nice shot!'—

'Beauty!'—never a quarrel about in or out. This behavior used
to make some people really mad, they said he was so god-
a'mighty Christian, so playing fields of Eton. Because, you
see, they knew he was out to win. He really and truly wanted
to win. He could put a dirty slice on the ball. But then with
me, alone, he was never mean or competitive—a million sur-
prises. Prankish, you know, suddenly at breakfast, 'God damn
it, Hazel, why is this toast buttered on the wrong side?' "

"Was it with you or with Maria that he moved out to the
country?"

"God help us, it was me. Southport, don't you remember?
You and Deborah were there. It was a divine house, but this
was the kind of thing, Hugh: there was this meadow in back,
it had been let go and was all grown up with underbrush, so
there was nothing for it but Moose had to buy a tractor with
a cutter bar. Hughie, he scared me; there was a kind of fury
about the way he had to keep that meadow cleared with that
horrible, dangerous slicing thing. His forebears stuck out all
over him. I began to understand stone walls for the first time.
The work! And such bleak work. And then, Hugh, he was
time-bound. He looked at his watch a thousand times a day,
every minute was important. This made for thrills, you know.
This big hulk would see a dewy spiderweb on the grass early
in the morning, and you had to go out on the lawn in your
bare feet and look at it with him at once, before it faded in
the sun. But the clock thing also led to a feeling he was wasting
time, not enjoying the minutes as much as he should have.
And what was so quirky about all that urgency was that it
somehow made him procrastinate to beat the band. He had
endless lists of things to do and never did them. It drove me
batty."

"What drove you to leave him? Was it the women?"

"For God's sake, Hugh," she said, suddenly sharp. "You
were his best friend. Why don't you let sleeping dogs lie?"

Moose had talked a lot over the years about Vance Talbot, who had served with him on the *Hornet*, and I'd met Talbot several times; he's a broker, very rich and very Reaganish now. The two were Ninety-Day Wonders—among the crop of lieutenants (junior grade), mostly just out of Ivy League colleges and mostly from "good families," as people used to say who thought that they were in them—who'd been given a crash course at Quonset and then been sent out to do non-combat duty of various kinds on carriers. I called Talbot, and he invited me to have a drink with him at the Harvard Club.

There was a hard sheen of newness on his blue pinstripe suit. He told about the crucial day in a bored, singsong voice; it was a memorized tale, almost worn out by retellings. "The second two torpedoes—from torpedo planes, you understand —hit at almost the same time, aft, and put the ship dead in the water. . . ." He must have known I wanted him to get to Moose, and he finally did. Three dive-bombers crashed onto the ship, he said, one on a slant into one side of the signal bridge—Moose's general-quarters station. "It was fantastic that he wasn't killed, the other three fellows up there were all ground up like hamburgers." I was beginning to find Talbot's narrative offensive. He must have seen me squirm. For my part, I could see that he was now enjoying himself. He dinged the table bell to order seconds on old-fashioneds for both of us.

But suddenly something shifted inside Talbot. He said, "Did Moose ever tell you about his terror?"

"He would never talk about the *Hornet*."

"Well, old boy," he said, "this was very deep in him. I got it out of him that night, on the destroyer that fished us out of the water. I was in awe of the man, because I kept seeing him, all day—he'd attached himself to Gowan, the exec, after the air department had left the ship, and he was toting Gowan's briefcase under the arm that had a big bloody first-aid bandage on it, and the two of them were all over the ship, you know. Jesus, the slaughter on the ranger deck was unbelievable, and truly scary fires, and the men in the engine room in a daze over their dead machinery—and these two were as cool and quiet as if they were checking in planes on a sunny day at air plot—words of encouragement, commands when they were needed, even bearing a hand on a bucket line or on the cable detail when that cruiser took us in tow. Moose being so big, this meant something. It helped gobs do what was expected of them. I was praising Moose for this stuff that night, and he looked at me like somebody who was on the moon and said that after the plane hit the signal deck, the next thing he knew he was two decks down, trying to open a sealed bulkhead door. He said—I remember he said—fear had struck him blind. So his total control after that, the ice in his veins, when he was tagging around with Gowan—those two chaps were the eye of the hurricane—was spooky."

All this was pronounced in those off-British north-shore-of-Long Island accents that people in the *Social Register* used to use. So was Talbot's reading of the lesson, which was not mine, as I thought later about his story. "It came to me that old Moose was off his rocker, you know. It affected him. For years. How else could you explain that whole Commie involvement? Someone with his background?"

The sybarite betrayed the saint; I suspect the saint prevented the sybarite from having as much fun as he would have liked. I always thought of Moose's womanizing as a concomitant, paradoxical as it may seem, of his New England decency. Probity was in his genes; he came from a line of citizens who had served at one time or another in two hundred years as preacher and teacher, as selectman, town counsel, village librarian, hayward, fence viewer, town meeting moderator, sheep-mark recorder, trainband ensign. He was deeply programmed with an urge to do the proper thing, and he very often did it, even where women were concerned—he married four of them, after all—but in the belly of the urge, one had to guess, there was something that had come down from Jonathan Edwards: a predisposition to, almost a yearning for, the threat of awful heat, a need to feel that he hung like a spider on a delicate but very strong thread, spun from his own body, over the fires in the pit. I doubt if he ever articulated or even recognized this need, if indeed he had it, but it was the only way I could glue him into one piece in my mind. I went to see Carol, Moose's third wife—the one Margot dismissed as having strayed a bit too much herself—and she said two things that interested me. "Moose didn't have an ounce of cruelty in him," she said, "but he was very attractive to masochistic women." And when we got on the subject of his unfaithfulness, she said quite coolly that sex with him was fantastic just after she had reason to think he'd cheated on her. Maybe the paradox in Moose was not just a matter of sex but cut all the way through him: the good sport at tennis with a dirty slice. He hated the war that had plucked his eyes out for an hour, yet it seemed that there was a warrior still and always embedded in him, fighting to win at any cost. And I wondered: As an attorney, was he everlastingly drawn to the underdog for good reasons, and perhaps for some not so good?

These thoughts homed in on me about three months later, when the Freedom of Information papers came through. I felt guilty reading them. I had the sneaky feeling of peeking at someone else's mail. I had to laugh at the number of words and lines and even pages that had been blacked out on the basis of a presumed danger to national security. From our Moose? There were several accounts of interviews in which the men in dark suits had questioned "subject Bradford" over and

over again on the associations leading to his defense of the
Communists in court, and what fascinated me in them was
the way the questioners repeatedly led Moose up to the edge
of naming names, and the way Moose, obviously tempted,
obviously knowing that had he done so the heat would have
been withdrawn, firmly pulled back each time, *toward* the
heat. But there were also passages that troubled me much
more, when the men in dark suits would themselves name the
names (most of them blotted out with black ink) and ask
subject Bradford his opinion of the named, and here, I'm sorry
to say, Moose didn't do so well. And here was where my
sensation of peeking, of poking into a neighbor's garbage in
search of some drab sign of his filth to hold against him, really
began to bother me. Because I began to wonder whether I
secretly wanted to dig up some dirt on my best friend, who
was dead.

But I read on. It was all sickening because it was all so
absurd. The agents' grammar was bad. They droned along—
insistent unanswerable questions. Now and then Moose got
angry, and you could see the prose of the agents' reports begin
to tremble with a fantasy of this gigantic Communist, as they
must have thought of him, suddenly charging at them with
the chopping motions of martial arts. Mostly, though, the
ritual was one of endless repetitions, circlings back, efforts to
entrap Moose into fatal contradictions. Then, at last, buried
in a long passage of humdrum miscellany, I found what I now
realize that in my heart of hearts I may have yearned to find.

The sentence was written in the flat, affectless tone of all
the rest. It simply said surveillance of Mildred Deming reported that at 23:15 p.m. on such-and-such date subject Bradford had checked in along with subject Deming at Moontop
Motor Inn in Torcottville, Virginia; register showed "Mr. and
Mrs. Winthrop Parsons." I was so riveted by the resonance of
this name he had chosen that for some time I didn't realize

the significance of the item. Then—Mildred Deming. Of course. I remembered. One of his possible associations during preparation of the defense of the Communists—one of the "known card carriers," as the men in dark suits kept calling them—that they had kept drumming at Moose about, over and over, only to meet repeated calm denials from him of ever having met this particular one.

I was deeply shocked by my realization of the importance of this buried item. For all those years I had been praising Moose to everyone for his integrity—for having had the courage to go to prison for his convictions—only to discover now that what had really put him in the noose with the FBI, and so of course with the Congressmen, was a "guilt by association" of the most sleazy sort, and his barefaced denials of it. A motel quickie. Moose had gone to prison for no better reason than that he had, in Margot's awful phrase, fooled around—this time (the moth drawn to the candle flame) with a doxy who happened to be a known card carrier.

That repulsive idea pushed me toward thoughts of Moose's death. The newspaper accounts of it had highlighted its irony. The irony that this famous lawyer, who had spent so much of his time on *pro bono publico* cases, who could have been far richer had he not defended so many adherents of unpopular causes, but also so many of the poor and so many of the sick, so many druggies and derelicts, so many of those lost in the murk of society's amnesia—the irony that this man should have been mugged to death on Madison Avenue at three o'clock in the morning by a little gang of those he seemed to have loved so much. The piece in the *Times* reported that a witness, a certain Morris Venabel, a short-order cook going home from his night shift at the Burgher's Burger at Madison and Seventy-third, had said that the victim, who was much larger than his three assailants, had first argued with them and then resisted. He had been stabbed just twice—in the back, as if to reinforce the irony. It had taken the witness ages to find a telephone at that hour, and by the time the police and an ambulance arrived, Bradford was dead on the sidewalk. I remember wondering, and then blaming myself for wondering, when I first read the report: Did Margot Bradford know where her husband had been at three o'clock that morning, before he started back to their pied-à-terre?

Walking down Madison on the way home from a dinner party a few nights after I read the FBI report—it was nearly midnight, and there were not many people around—I felt jumpy and out of sorts. There had been some conversation about Moose at dinner, and Fay Callender, who hardly knew him, had gone on and on in a whining voice about what a good man he was. She had got on my nerves, and I had drunk too much red wine. Now, as I walked along, I suddenly found myself drafting in my mind an account of Moose's death for my piece. I visualized the scene. I would be the witness Venabel.

Here came this tall, well-built man, refreshed by what he'd been up to. Maybe a lone taxi would have gone uptown just then, and in the quick wash of its headlights I would see the gray suit, the arms swinging, the long lope of the pace. Then, as he reached a relatively dim stretch halfway between streetlights, three men jumped out from the recess of the entrance to an antique store. They were ahead of him, they blocked his way. One of them had something black and shiny in his hand, which might have been a water pistol—or a Saturday-night special. I couldn't hear the words, but all three of these people, who were dwarfed by the man they had stopped, were jabbering at once. The man held up his hand in a stopping signal, said something. In my imagination I now came closer. Was he telling them he was their friend? They hooted and made demands. I imagined that I saw, he must have seen, a new glint of steel.

It was here, as I think back on it, that my reconstruction of the mugging began to go haywire. I thought I heard my best friend Moose lecturing the muggers in a loud voice now, telling them they should be ashamed of themselves, they were a disgrace to their class of people, and to their families. Did he realize, as he tried to save his own life, that he had summoned up for these hooligans the stern voice of all the generations, standing behind him, of upright men? Whether he did or not, that voice, which seemed to come to my ears as if from the pulpit, rattled me. I began to be terribly afraid. At first I had imagined that I was watching, that I was the man Venabel. But now I was horrified to find that I might be, in my imagination, one of the three attackers. He was lecturing *me*. Perhaps I had a weapon in my hand, I certainly had one in my mind. I imagined that I was shouting along with the other two. I could hear my voice crack as I asked, "When was 'that time' with Deb? Come on, Moose, old cock, tell me, you'd better tell me." I didn't want to hurt him— Moose, Moose, my best and only friend—but I felt that I might not be able to control what my hand might do. I was seared by the heat of my own anger. He denied and denied. What "time" was I talking about? There was no such "time." This was all some fiction of Margot's. I shouted that he was a liar, a liar. . . .

When I got home, I poured myself a drink, and gradually I calmed down. I don't know what o'clock it was when I went to my desk, gathered all the notes I'd made on the Moose piece and took them into the kitchen and dropped them into the refuse chute, from which there was no possibility of recovery.

The Captain

We were on deck making up gear that morning, tied up to Dutcher's Duck opposite Poole's, when the new hand came aboard. Caskie, the skipper, seated on an upended bucket, was stitching some new bait bags, his huge, meaty fingers somehow managing to swoop the sail needle with delicate feminine undulations in and out of the bits of folded net. You could buy bait bags, but would Caskie? He had a closed face, signifying nothing. We knew he must have been hurt by Manuel Cautinho, who had served him as mate nineteen long years and had suddenly walked off on him, but there was no reading Caskie's face, any more than you could read the meditations of a rock awash at high tide off Gay Head. His was a tight-sealed set of features, immobile and enigmatic in their weather-cracked hide. His eyes were downcast, the hoods of the lids the color of cobwebs, unblinking as he steadily worked. We never knew what he thought; sometimes we wondered if he ever needed to think.

I had been bowled over with the luck of being given a site as shacker on Caskie Gurr's *Gannet*. I was an apprentice, I got all the dirty work, I was salting stinking remains of pogies and yellowtail for bait with a foul tub between my feet that morning, but it didn't matter. (You could buy frozen bait, but . . .) Caskie had the best reputation of any of the offshore lobstering skippers out of either Menemsha or New Bedford. Everyone said that he cared, more than most, whether his men got decent shares, and that he knew, better than most, the track of the seasonal marches of the lobbies on the seabed of the shelf out there. *Gannet* was known as a wise boat. Caskie's regulars had been three senior islanders, who had been with him through a great deal of dusty weather—till Cautinho walked off for no apparent reason.

Pawkie Vincent, the engineer, sat far aft rigging a new trawl flag on a high-flyer—a marker buoy with a radar reflector on it, for one end of a line of pots. Pawkie had only nine fingers, yet he was so deft with them that it sometimes seemed he had three hands. He had lost the index finger of his right hand when it got mashed, one time, while he was shipping the steel-bound doors of a dragging net. Every once in a while as he worked, he would shake his head slightly from side to side, as if some troublesome doubt had occurred to him. Pawkie was tentative; his pauses to think things out in moments of intricate teamwork were sometimes dangerous to the rest of us.

The cook, Drum Jones, was fastening bricks into some new oak pots that had not yet become waterlogged, to hold them in place on the bottom. He had, beneath a railroad engineer's cap, the gaunt face of someone who has seen a ghost, and he sported an odd little mustache that looked like a misplaced eyebrow and accentuated his habitual look of alarm. This made it all the more surprising that he was always cheerful, always optimistic. When we pulled up a lean trawl of pots, he'd always say the next string would be better. But it seldom had been on recent trips—so Drum's dogged good humor was often annoying.

No one had much to say that morning. Our shares had been

slim of late. Pawkie, who had a cranky wife and three wild sons in high school, had said that except for the shame of it, his family would do a damn sight better on welfare. I was an outsider, but I could see that Cautinho's departure had suddenly ruptured a brotherhood of these older men, a closeness rich with memories of many years of risks and scrapes and injuries and quarrels, to say nothing of a never-mentioned pride in the way they had handled together their very hard life under the discipline of their cruel and inscrutable mother, the sea. They were laconic. The only words they used were about tasks. Their tongues could not possibly have given passage to nouns like "trust," "endurance," "courage," "loyalty," or, God forbid, "love." What stood in jeopardy now, with Cautinho gone, leaving a gap like that of a pulled tooth, was the sense of the serene and dependable teamwork *Gannet's* crew had enjoyed, the delicate meshing of Caskie's understated but revered and absolute captaincy with the known capacities— and weaknesses, such as Pawkie's hesitations—of the other three, all working together as parts of an incarnate machine, each one knowing exactly what was expected of him and what the others could and would and wouldn't do in moments of critical stress. One linchpin was gone now out of that smooth-running machine, and I couldn't help wondering if it might fly apart under the strain of breaking in a new man. But of course no one could talk about any of that.

There was another thing we couldn't talk about: The Company. That meant Sandy Persons, the owner of *Gannet*. Persons, a sharp little creature, only about thirty years old, in a snap-brimmed felt hat and a double-breasted suit and what looked to us like custom-made shoes, *was* The Company. He reputedly owned six draggers, ours out of Menemsha and the others based in New Bedford. I was aware of the hushed voices with which Pawkie and Drum and Cautinho had always talked about Persons, each time we steamed into New Bedford and tied up and unloaded our catch, after which Caskie walked off with Persons to settle up—our captain shuffling away on the stone pier with a slack pace and a bowed head. The crewmen's voices were muffled then, I inferred, by their sense of Caskie's everlasting humiliation that he couldn't afford to be his own man on his own boat; that he was just another captain on broken-forty shares with a company embodied in this little peewee, who, we suspected, in our conspiratorial sympathy for Caskie, could not really be the owner but must be some kind of mob underling. We had a sense that vast, unfair, and probably crooked forces controlled our lives. You could never read on Caskie's face, when he returned from those conferences, how he felt about this little muskrat of an owner, and you certainly wouldn't dare ask him.

We worked in silence that morning. It was a hot September day, with fog burning away to silvery haze before noon. Our heads were lowered over our jobs. All four of us were startled by a sudden thump, and our downturned eyes swept the deck to see its cause—a backpack thrown down onto it from the dock.

"Cap'n Gurr?" a voice asked.

I looked up and saw a fair imitation of Goliath. That package of beef would certainly have no trouble fetching the pots in over the side as they came up from the deep. This was our new mate. He had a big red beard, full lips, a nose as wide as a fist set in cheerful ruddy cheeks. But it seemed to me that there were empty places where the eyes should have been. You could not tell, looking at those hollows, that he was *there*. There was a flicker of something like a smile—or was it?—tucked in his beard around his mouth. My first thought was: He's on something. This isn't going to work.

But Caskie said, "I'm glad to see you. Come aboard."

His name was Benson, he wanted to be called Ben. He'd heard about the site on *Gannet* from someone at Poole's, and

Caskie, in need of a hand, had accepted him over the phone. This was the first time the skipper had laid eyes on the man. Caskie had told us that Benson said he'd served in the fishery off Nova Scotia—out of Lunenburg, Port Medway, Sydney, Ingonish; rough, cold, sloppy work, the fellow must have liked it. Now Caskie's unreadable eyes searched Benson's vacant ones, and all Caskie said was "We're shaping up to go out tonight. Bear a hand, would you?" He set Benson to splicing gangions into a new groundline—the short lengths of rope, branching off at intervals from the mile-long line of a trawl, to which individual pots would be tied. Not another word between them. I guess Caskie wanted to see if Benson knew anything. He did. His splices were perfect.

When we'd finished our chores about noontime, Caskie said he'd tune in to the 5 p.m. weather forecast, and if it sounded all right he'd telephone to each of us to come aboard. Pawkie and Drum went to their houses, and I to the stark roost I had rented in West Tisbury with a couple of other young adventurers, whose rites of passage involved hammers, Skilsaws, stapling guns. Benson stayed aboard; had no place to go, he said.

At suppertime, Caskie phoned and said the weather report was, as he put it, "on the edge of all right," and he guessed we'd better take our chances and go out—the trawls had been set out there for nearly two weeks as it was. That statement had, wrapped in the folds of its succinctness, an unspoken rebuke to the vanished Cautinho for having caused several days' delay while Caskie filled his site. I was young and brash, and before Caskie hung up I asked, "Is the new man going to be okay?"

I should have known better. There was a long, long pause—which I took to have a meaning: Mind your own business. "We'll see," he finally said.

When we got to the boat, I heard Pawkie murmur to Drum

that he'd listened to the forecast, too, and he said, "Some real dirty stuff's comin' through tomorrer—wind backin' to nawtheast, twenty to thirty."

"It'll be fine," Drum said. "Cask wouldn't do anythin' dumb."

We cast off at 9 p.m. sharp, glided out between the jetties, and steamed into the wide bight under a sky that was like a great city of lights. At first, a moderate southwest breeze gently rocked our fat-bellied *Gannet* as if she were a cradle. Then we rounded up into those mild airs and made for the open ocean. The big diesel Cat in the boat's guts hummed. I was off watch until midnight, but I stayed out on the afterdeck until we rounded Gay Head and I could know, peering out ahead over the rail, that there was nothing but the vast reach of the sea between our tiny vessel and magical faraway anchorages of my imagination: Bilbao, Lisbon, Casablanca. I felt free out beyond Gay Head and Noman's, on the wide waters of infinity, free from all the considerations ashore that tied one down—telephones, groceries, laundry, parents, the evening news, and, yes, even friends—free to exist without thinking, free to be afraid only of things that were really fearful. That last was a great gift of the sea. I filled my lungs, over and over, with air that I imagined was redolent, thanks to the great sweep of a dying fair-weather high, of the sweet flowers of Bermuda. After a while I went below and plunged into sleep in my clothes.

Caskie, who had taken the first watch to set our course solidly for our trawl lines, waked me at eight bells, and I took my turn in the pilothouse. *Gannet* steered herself, on auto, into the void. There was not much to do: check the compass now and then, take a turn on deck every half hour just to make sure that all was secure—and, well, you couldn't call the gradual emptying of my mind daydreaming; it was dark out.

The skipper had assigned our new mate the dawn watch. I went down at 3:50 a.m. and put a hand on a big round arm, which felt as solid as a great sausage, and shook it. Benson came roaring up out of sleep, looming and pugnacious, his hands fisted, as if he'd had to spend his whole life defending himself. Then he evidently realized where he was and went limp on the bunk for a minute with his mouth open and working, drinking consciousness until he was full enough to get up. I went back to the pilothouse, and when he turned up, right on time, I showed where things were—loran, radar, radio, switches, fuses, button for the horn, all the junk. There was a small round seat on a stanchion behind the wheel, like a tall mushroom, and Benson heaved himself up on it and perched there in a massive Buddha's calm. I still couldn't find him in his eyes, but I'd obviously been wrong: he couldn't have been drugged. He understood, he could deal with the electronics, he had handled the marlinspike when he was splicing with an old-time sailmaker's precision.

"What happened with the other mate?" he asked me. His voice was mild and rather high-pitched, as if he housed an inner person who was less assertive, less rough-cut, than the exterior one. He wanted to know how come he had lucked into this site.

"He just up and left," I said.

"I heard a rumor, some guy at Poole's," Ben said. "Somethin' about the guy was fed up with the cap'n hangin' on to lobsterin' when all the rest of 'em give up and switched over to draggin'. Said the cap'n was stubborn as a stone."

"I wouldn't know," I said.

"Said the cap'n was a peddler. Wasn't no lobsters out there."

"We've been getting a few," I said.

Ben gave a resounding snort, deep and haunting, as if he had a conch shell for a nose. I felt uncomfortable hearing such words about the captain behind his back, and I sidled out of there and went below. But I got only an hour's sleep, because Caskie had risen around five and, as usual, had steamed straight to the loran fix of his first trawl, south of the steamer lanes in fifty fathoms of water, on the shelf about midway between Block Canyon and Atlantis Canyon. He had picked up the radar buoy on the scope in no time, and had sent Ben down to roust the rest of us out.

The wind had freshened from the sou'west, and we were rolling. I pulled on my oilers and my metal-toed boots. *Gannet* had been converted from a seventy-two-foot Gulf shrimper, and her cedar planks clung to oak ribs that had been steam-bent to make a belly as round as a bait tub, unlike the deep-keeled draggers built for northern waters, so to tell the truth she wasn't too sea-kindly. She wallowed in broadside waves. Caskie had gone down to Key West nineteen years ago and bought her for The Company for twenty thousand dollars; she'd be worth ten times that now. He'd had her hauled and done some work on her, and she was sound, though her white-painted topsides were grimy, chipped, and rust-streaked, and her bulwarks were draped with old tires, so she looked like an aging hooker of the sea. Who cared? Inboard she was roomier than the North Atlantic draggers, and we thought we lived in style. Pawkie called her "the Georgie's Bank Hilton."

In the gray half-light we were on deck trying to adjust our land legs to the argumentative gravity of the sea. Caskie came out to con the boat and run the hydraulic hauler from the auxiliary controls, abaft the deckhouse on the starboard side. He was cool. He swung the boat into the eye of the wind with his usual skill, as if it were a toy in a tub, and eased up alongside the aluminum staff of the radar buoy marking the western end of the string. We were pitching a bit in the seaway, and Ben, in his first chore as bulwarkman, missed a grab at the flag with a gaff. Pawkie was standing by with a grappling hook in case it was needed, and he made as if to toss it, but Ben waved him off and, leaning out over the rail, managed to catch the staff. He hoisted it aboard, Drum detached the end line and served it through a block hung from the starboard boom, Pawkie fed the line into the hydraulic lift, Caskie started the winch, and we were in business. The half-inch polypropylene rope snaked and hissed through the sheaves of the hauler and coiled itself on the deck underneath it.

When the anchor of the end line came up—a sturdy bucket full of concrete, a hundred-pound weight—Benson lifted it aboard and stowed it as easily as if it were made of styrofoam. Finally the first pot appeared. Not a single lobster. Pawkie groaned. Benson heaved the heavy oaken trap on board with a power in the shoulders and a look of anger in the face that gave me a shiver. He detached the pot from its becket with a snort like the one I had heard from him in the night, when I'd said we were catching "a few." After that we were all herky-jerky, retrieving this first string of pots. Big Ben knew what he was doing, all right, and he had strength to burn, but Pawkie and Drum didn't know his moves, and they kept semi-interfering in efforts to ensure the continuity of rhythms that are a must in hauling pots. Each time they leaned or reached toward Benson to lend a hand, he shook them off with a guttural sound that wasn't quite speech and wasn't quite a growl, whereupon they fell back and got out of sync on what they were supposed to do next themselves.

The harvest was miserable. A good-sized but lonely lobbie now and then, and a few eels and crabs and trash fish—which we would keep and sell in New Bedford. My job was to peg, which in our case meant slipping rubber bands over the claws, and half the time I just stood around and waited. Caskie looked grim. From thirty pots in that first trawl we gleaned only twelve lobsters.

Drum served us breakfast after that trawl. Caskie stayed in

the pilothouse. We ate silently. Toward the end of the string I had noticed that a human presence had finally made its appearance in Ben's eyes, and that the persona of that presence was a peckish human being who had decided to hate our captain. It struck me that the eyes had been dead until bad blood infused them with a sparkling life. Between pots those eyes threw laser beams at Caskie. Everyone knows that there is a noble tradition, among seagoing men, of hating the captain. Captain-hating, even of good captains, goes very far back; the animals in the ark probably hated Noah, even though he was saving them from drowning. There were two troubles here. One was that Pawkie and Drum had learned over many years, perhaps not without pain, how not to hate Caskie—who would dare utter the word "love"?—and I could sense that there had been some mute emotional transactions going on out there on the deck between the old hands and Ben, which were as threatening as the turbulent dark clouds that had begun to loom over the landward horizon. The other was that this guy who had showed up in the hollows of Big Ben's eyes looked like a born spoiler, who didn't belong on a cockleshell of a boat out on the open sea.

The crazy thing was that when we started pulling up the next trawl, all five of us began working in perfect teamwork, with the marvelous harmonies of a string quintet playing "The Trout." The gang meshed better than it had when Cautinho was aboard. As each pot came up, Caskie stopped the hauler; Big Ben reached out and swung the trap aboard and guided it onto the rail and untied it from its gangion; Caskie re-engaged the hauler to bring up the next trap; Ben and Drum pushed the pot along the rail to the picking station; Pawkie opened it and, first off, stabbed eels that were trapped and dumped them writhing into the eel barrel; he and I dropped the lobbies, if any, in the lobster tank, the trash onto the culling table, and the crabs into the fish box; Drum rebaited the pot; Ben slid it aft along the rail and stacked it while Drum, standing at the culling table, threw eggers—females with roe—and shorts—sexually immature ones—overboard; I began banding; Pawkie threw the gurry into the sea and cleaned up; then we'd all be ready to receive the next trap. If anything got the slightest bit out of rhythm, perhaps after one of Pawkie's hesitations, the guys would spontaneously jump to shift jobs without anything said. It was miraculous. It was as if this disdainful muscleman had been on the boat forever, and all of us could see that the smoothness of our work originated in his skill and alacrity—and anger. Whenever a pot would come up empty, the sounds in his throat now shaped themselves as words: "Shit, not again!" or, "Jesus, man," or, "I can't *believe* this."

Caskie said he had decided not to reset the trawls in that lobster-forsaken area; he said he would wait and set them "inside"—in shallower water north of the ship lanes. "I should hope so," Benson muttered. But as we resumed hauling, in the third and fourth strings, as the stack of empty traps built up on the afterdeck, the catch was a bit better—seemed to be improving as we followed the sets out to the eastward. Meanwhile, the wind had indeed begun to back around, as Pawkie had said it would, and had freshened; it was out of the east at that point. We had to widen our stance on the deck to keep from staggering around. As we got into the fourth trawl, *Gannet* was pitching like a hobbyhorse, the pots swung ominously from the boom when they came up, and the many hundred-pound traps tied down in a big stack athwartships strained dangerously at their lashings.

By the time we had shipped all the traps from that trawl, the wind was snarling in from the northeast with its teeth bared, chewing the tops off eight-foot seas. There was a gale brewing. Caskie, with his long habit of consultation with his gang, said, "How about it? Shall we pack it in?"

"Jesus cripes," Benson shouted into the wind, "just when you're catchin' a few?" His echo of my words in the night gave me the shudders. But now when I think about it, I realize that what really shook me was Benson's challenge to everything that I thought of as valuable in an orderly life. His tone of voice was a threat to the very idea of captaincy. Caskie was a mild island man of a certain age; he consulted out of courtesy but always made his decisions entirely on his own, and the serenity we had enjoyed when Cautinho was aboard, though possibly false, had rested squarely on the dependability of Caskie's gentle authority. He had always got us back safely to Menemsha basin. Now this raw Benson had come down here off Newfoundland's bitter waters to break the contract seamen invariably make, whether they like it or not, with skipperhood. You can hate a captain, but you obey him nevertheless. This wasn't a generational thing; I was far closer to Big Ben's age than to Caskie's, but I had been raised to a reasoned life, and I think I was more frightened of mutiny than I was of drowning.

Caskie, his expressionless face soaked with spray, looked at Benson for a long time. "All right," he finally said. "One more string, then we'll see." I was shocked by his yielding, and I saw Pawkie and Drum both literally step back away from Benson on the deck, as if he had raised a fist against them.

"Maybe it's just a squall," Drum stupidly said, so desirous of peace aboard *Gannet* that he lost all touch with mother wit.

You could hear, over the wind raking the rigging, that conch shell of a nose in a wild snort of derision.

Caskie had gone into the pilothouse to steam us to the next flag. It seemed to take us forever to get there. And sure enough, after a while, he came out on the careening deck and called out to us over the wind, "Flag ain't there."

"Damn Russians!" Pawkie shouted.

Of all times for this to happen! We always blamed snagged or lost trawls on the Russians, though there were also Japanese, German, Polish, Italian—and maybe Spanish, maybe Bulgarian—and probably other—vessels out there, huge factory ships with satellite boats dragging enormous nets on the bottom, ripping up the ecology of the shelf, slaughtering all God's species with a greed and rapacity that gave no thought to times to come. And ruining puny us, sure enough. Anytime we lost a whole string of forty pots—and it had happened more than once—The Company was out a couple of thousand bucks, and we were that much nearer to being out of work.

Caskie shouted that he was going to steam out to look for the tide balls at the other end of the busted line; maybe some of the pots could be salvaged. He went back in the pilothouse.

Pawkie was shaking his head. "How you going to find those damn floats in this shit?"

"Caskie'll find 'em," Drum said, putting his whole heart into his hoping.

And this time Drum was right. Caskie did. The fat hull pounded and shivered and wallowed out to the eastward. I was the first to see the orange spheres playing hide-and-seek in the spume-capped waves, and I called out the bearing at the pilothouse door. Caskie eased up to them. Out on deck Pawkie picked up the grappling iron and its line, but Benson grabbed it away from him and on a single throw caught one of the tide-ball lines and pulled the rope aboard. With all the strength of his anger, Benson got the first ball on deck, and then the second. By this time Caskie was again at the auxiliary controls, and between them Pawkie and Drum fed the end line into the winch sheaves.

"Somethin's wrong," Caskie said right away. The end line was skidding and laboring in the sheaves. It came up slowly. Caskie had brought *Gannet*'s bow up into the wind, and she was bucking like a bronco in a rodeo with burrs under its saddle. Each time her fat forefoot crashed down into a trough, a ton of spray flew up over the pilothouse and cascaded down on us, icy and stinging, like deliberate and repeated warnings from an ocean scandalized by our folly.

When the last twenty feet came up, we saw that the end line had somehow become tangled and twisted with the bottom trawl line, so that the bucket of cement that had anchored the end line and one of the pots had risen together. No sooner had they cleared the waves than those two lethal objects began spinning around each other as the ropes they were hanging from worked to untwist themselves.

Seeing the danger to his men at once, Caskie braked the lift and, depending on a friend he had worked with through many a hazard, shouted, "Pawk! Get the long gaff and try to hook the pot."

"No!"

It was not a shout, it was a roar. We all froze—or at least, as I look back, I see us immobilized in a still picture of that terrible moment of disobedience. Benson had his hands raised in a stopping gesture, as if to beat back the captain's command. Pawkie already had the gaff, with its murderous hook lifted and aimed out over the bulwarks, in his two hands. Drum was in a kind of crouch, as if to dodge some physical blow against the accepted way of doing things that he could sense but could not believe. Caskie stood with his hands on the conning controls, his face all too readable for the first time I could ever remember. I saw rage there, and I saw knowledge, and I saw defeat—the defeat of a quiet man whose calmness had its footing on a set of old, old rules of the sea, always accepted on *Gannet* until that very instant, the most important of which was that a word from the commanding officer in a tight moment is not to be questioned. The first law of the sea: The captain *is* the ship. He had yielded once, and I saw on his face that he would give in now. In the still picture that hangs on in my mind, *Gannet* herself was poised in a tremble of horror on a high crest, and the concrete weight and the lobster pot, spinning around each other, were making a dreadful blur of the reality to which the big mate had attached his defiance.

Then Ben made his move. With a lunge he snatched the gaff from Pawkie's hands and threw it away on the deck. Next, with breathtaking disregard for the danger, he leaned his body out over the rail and snatched the end line in his left hand, just above the fast-moving handle of the bucket of concrete. He was very nearly pulled overboard by the momentum of that hurtling weight, but he managed to hook himself to the rail with his right hand and a bent knee. The spinning stopped. The deck lurched on the crest of a big wave. Ben took advantage of *Gannet*'s plunge and heaved the weight over the rail and onto the deck. The lobster pot came in easily then. It had several big ones in it.

We got in four more pots, and that was all. The trawl had been cut. We headed for home.

In a marvel of balance in the galley as *Gannet* steeply lurched up each wave and then dropped in what seemed a free-fall until it hit the rock bottom of the ensuing trough, then rose shuddering again on the next vicious sea, Drum fried four eggs for each of us. Pawkie was on watch. Caskie sat down to his lunch across from Big Ben. I was at the end of the table, and Drum was cleaning up. As if we were floating on a dead calm, Caskie began to speak in a quiet and respectful voice to the man who had countermanded his order and made a success of it, and my heart sank as I listened to his appeasement of Benson. Big Ben gave no answers; eating, he made grunting sounds.

"I don't think you understand," Caskie said. "The Company says, 'Keep on lobsterin',' and you've got no choice. They own you, don't you know. I told Persons, I said, 'It's all over for lobsters out there this year, we ought to go to draggin',' but he says, 'We got to have lobsters, we're gettin' all the yellowtail an' fluke and scup we can handle from the other boats, we need lobsters.' If I say my gang can't make a livin', he says well, it's tough titty, he can get other skippers, he can get other guys for crews. I said I'd been on my boat for nineteen years, I didn't like that kind o' talk, and believe me, Mr. Benson, he blew up, he used language I wouldn't repeat to you. He was extremely definite, you know. Extremely."

It was horrible. The sweet sap of command had been drained right out of Caskie, and now all he had left was his impressive New England decency, which was taking the form of groveling. Benson didn't even look up at his captain. He had egg on his beard. I felt seasick and had to go up on deck.

I don't know what happened after that. I asked Drum, when we got ashore, but he just shook his head. We tied up in New Bedford after midnight, and Benson heaved his backpack up on the dock and climbed ashore and walked off. When we got back to Menemsha, Pawkie quit. I hated to do it after six trips, but I had to tell Caskie that I thought I wasn't going to make it at sea, I didn't have good sea legs, I thought I'd try carpentry.

Caskie said, "Good luck, son. Don't take any wooden nickels." I couldn't for the life of me tell from his face whether he was glad or sorry to have me go.

Mr. Quintillian

One morning in late April of a year toward the end of the Depression, I decided to walk to work. The sky was blue, and the early light was pressing against the buildings with the urgency of the sun when May and June are coming soon, as if the buildings were dormant and could be brought by warmth of the right sort to bud and to leaf. When I stepped out of the damp entryway of my walk-up, I saw this importunate sunlight against the structures higher up, probing the brick and sooty stone as though there must surely be life hidden in the winter-deadened walls. I paused on the corner to catch my usual bus, and there, as I turned to face the curb, this sunlight flooded my forehead and cheeks—I wore no hat—and I felt a burst of energy, and I decided to walk. I started across town.

I was not, strictly speaking, elated. Money and Mr. Quintillian were on my mind.

The sunlight may have impelled my walking to begin with, but I am bound to say that my pace was quickened, as I moved along the sidewalks, less by a feeling that the sap was rising in me than by a satisfaction that I was saving a nickel by not taking a bus. The last thing before going to bed each night, I jotted in a book my outlay for the day, and each evening the little pattern of figures made me sad, as if I had drawn a picture of a wreck. I loved money and I wanted much more of it than I had: I had very little at all. My idea of beauty was the engraving on the margins of a dollar bill, the delicate curves swelling and petering out like luck itself. As I walked I glared at the costly stuff in the store windows. The second button was off my topcoat, and I pulled at the threads that just the day before had given up their long, weary grip on the disk of imitation bone, but I could not work them free of the cloth, so I rolled them into a tight swirl and hoped that as the other buttons held the coat in place the threads would not be seen. I slowed my pace, remembering that this was only the second day I had worn the shirt I had on, and that an incautious pace might make it unwearable another day; laundry money was my despair.

Mr. Quintillian was my ultimate despair because he stood, as it were, between me and money. Our floor at the office was arranged as a sort of honeycomb of stalls, or cubicles, with waist-high plaster walls topped by barriers of crinkled glass that did not reach the ceiling. The noises of typewriters and adding machines and men and women talking on telephones rose from these glass boxes and hovered and mixed overhead in a low-hanging vapor of confusion. It was my fate to share a cubicle with Mr. Quintillian, the head of our department. Each Friday afternoon he opened the big strongbox on his desk and began counting out and putting into envelopes the week's wages for all the people on our floor, and I had to sit there listening to the dry whisper of bills and the tinkle of coins as with the dexterity and apparently absentminded swiftness of a woman knitting he went through the roster of payees and doled out the right sum for each. At last he put all the envelopes in a wire basket. There were no names on them. He knew which was which, and he never made a mistake. He started with me as being nearest at hand, flicking his long

fingers into the basket and pulling my envelope out and handing it to me with his lips pursed and not a word, as if spending
salary money on the likes of me would surely mean the decline
and end of a solid old business to which he had given thirty-
four years of his thin-blooded life. He would shake his head
and leave our stall and begin the round of the floor, handing
out company money and looking as though it devastated him
to do so.

The despair that any thought of Mr. Quintillian stirred up
in me was that there might never be enough money. He was
my opposite, I thought—old, desiccated, and futureless—yet
he was also the spectacle of a future I might, if I was not wary,
have to confront myself one day. In my mind I was just a kid
passing through his department, training, getting the experience that would go into the broad view of some sort of
manager who would have an office on a higher floor, so I
resented Mr. Quintillian as a reminder that I might, to the
contrary, become stuck in his noisy honeycomb, that in fact
I might be training to become another he. On his side, he
resented me, I am sure, because he saw my arrogation, saw
that I was not dedicated to the picayune life of his department.
He knew that I thought I was too big for his britches; this
led to a definite coolness.

Mr. Quintillian owned an ancient green celluloid eyeshade,
which he wore as though he worked not under the most up-
to-the-minute egg-crated fluorescent lighting, which our office
had, but rather under the down-thrown stare of ancient, primitive naked bulbs of clear glass with little spikes where the
vacuum had been sealed off. We swam about in a bath of
warm, benign luminosity, but his eyes seemed to need a private
home in shadows. His head was bald and had a sharp glistening
bump at the top, and his forehead above the eyeshade was
sallow and deeply lined. Mr. Quintillian was precise. He drew
clean, tidy lines with a steel ruler as he worked; he had a huge,

clanking adding machine with a crank, on which he checked computations after doing them in his head; and he made neat little stacks of papers on his desk, which he all but aligned with a carpenter's square. He kept his records in longhand, in minute calligraphic figures. He seemed to want to be a machine; he was one jump ahead of automation, practicing it in his inner works. He had lost a tooth too far back in his mouth for the gap to be seen when he talked, and occasionally he sucked audibly at its socket as if that were where he stored the sweetmeats of his life.

A stoplight held me at a corner. A cabbie wearing a dirty plaid cap and tremendously thick glasses, which made his eyes look like toy headlights, shouted from his window at a starchy, pale motorist from out of town who had crowded him: "Look what drives cars around these days."

The visitor to the city clamped his teeth tight, biting an answer, and looked straight ahead.

What an angry city!

As I walked on, anger turned over in its sleep in me; I felt myself blush, thinking again of Mr. Quintillian, because I had overheard him talking unkindly about me at the office two or three days before. This was not something I had imagined. It had been out at the typists' bullpen, where Mr. Quintillian hovered, as thin and twitchy as a dragonfly, beside the heaped desk of Miss Parch, the head typist, a co-survivor with himself of many long years in the firm and the only person he was ever seen to honor with a smile—a drawing back of the lips, that is, which seemed to express some marvelous satisfaction he shared with her, such as "Well! Things are certainly going badly today, aren't they?" I came up to him from behind, my gum-rubber soles squeaking on the waxed floor no louder than the space bar of one of the typewriters, and Mr. Quintillian was hissing to Miss Parch that I would not last long, and he specified a reason: slovenly. Mind, body, and desk. He seemed very glad. I put down my papers in Miss Parch's in-basket, and when he saw me his eyebrows shot up under his green eyeshade like a pair of park squirrels startled to cover by a dangerous intruder. He bared his amber teeth to Miss Parch and turned away.

I knew that he might be right. I had heard that Mr. Quintillian's past cubicle-sharers had been famous for nothing but the speed with which they got fired. No one in that cramped little glass box ever seemed to "measure up." If I couldn't measure up to a Quintillian's standards, how in the world would I ever acquire "enough" money?

Money such as Charley Force had. He was one of my two apartment-mates. He was younger than I, yet he seemed to buy something of quality every day, while I pressed my mind for ways of not buying anything. We three, on the top floor of a creaky old house in the East Thirties, were recent college graduates, getting started, vaguely expecting to marry sometime and, as they would say, settle down. We had two rooms, and because Force was the longest-standing tenant, he drew one of them in which to sleep alone. He was heavy-bearded and, despite morning shaves, looked dissolute by suppertime. A few days before, he had bought a new item on the market, an electric razor, and now every time I cut my face shaving with razor blades dulled by economizing, I cursed Charley Force's unearned, as well as his earned, income.

In the next block, I thought of the face of the new girl who had recently come to work in Mr. Quintillian's department. She seemed sympathetic; her smile was timid, and I fancied that she had looked sorry for me, for some reason, the one time our eyes had met. She wore her bright hair in braids coiled like a coronet. I had a feeling she was not a sound sleeper, because the places under her eyes were faintly bluish and seemed almost transparent. In a week I had not heard her voice, and in a whole year to come, I realized, I might not—

she was off at a far corner of the floor. Someone had said her name was Miss Tammer.

Charley Force would savvy what to do about such a girl. Only the night before, he had packed me and our third fellow lodger, Manny Dran, out to the movies, so he could be alone with his current flame in our apartment. Charley actually used the word "flame"; the desire Manny and I had to burn the place down when he dealt with us that way was keen. Our rooms were like those of a dormitory in some shabby backwater college. One of the beds in the room Manny and I shared had a brass frame, and the other, on which I slept, was a lumpy day couch. We had two dark old oaken bureaus and always a heap of empty beer bottles in a wastebasket. Charley Force's room was a sophomore heaven, with an elaborate Telefunken radio, whose bands, he said, would pick up Peking, Calcutta, and Sydney, and with two suffocating stuffed chairs, both pushed against clanking radiators, so that sitting in them was like reclining in a crater in a midsummer sand dune. On the two walls there were never-explained enlarged photographs of a barren hillside and of a Fall River night steamer, and in the windows hung dirty white curtains with bunting-like gathers at the tops that Charley Force, from somewhere in his fussy background, called "matching priscillas." The apartment had brown walls. This miserable room of his filled me with envy.

I walked along thinking these thoughts. But soon I eased up. What a promising day! The air was like ginger ale.

I was astonished, on my arrival at work, to swing around the partition into the cubicle I shared with Mr. Quintillian and to surprise him in close and secretive conversation with the new girl. I surprised him, all right. At his first view of my refreshed face, Mr. Quintillian raised his hands somewhat as a desert horse lifts his forelegs at the shock a rattlesnake's buzzer gives it, one above the other, very grandly, a caracole, and as he abruptly raised his head toward me with bared granivorous teeth, the green eyeshade slipped from it with a dry, thin rustling to the floor. Miss Tammer promptly bent over to pick it up, and I was struck by an aspect of her I had not before noticed, for she was wearing a thin dress in honor of the first warmish day of spring; she was plump in places. Her face had not particularly advertised this. Her blush when she straightened up, perhaps merely a consequence of her considerate plunge for the eyeshade, which must have thrown blood into her head, and the deference, subservience, with which she put into Mr. Quintillian's blue-veined hand the glistening leftover from an era she and I could only have known through old silent movies—faithful stationmaster, with garters holding up his sleeves, tapping at the telegraph key to warn of the approach of Number 93, which has been misswitched and is headed straight for the dynamited bridge at Simmons' Gap—those signs, as well as his cursory nod when he took the eyeshade from her, a gesture not so much of thanks as dismissal, made me wonder what in the world had been going on. The whole swift transaction seemed to me to give fascinating hints of intimacy, if not, in fact, of conspiracy.

The next thing I knew, her skirt was flicking out of there, and Mr. Quintillian was clearing his throat with a whole series of little laryngeal pushes, which I took as earnestly as if the words had been written in blood across Mr. Quintillian's gleaming forehead, to utter this message: Young man, a shut mouth helps one to get ahead.

It was very queer. I had had an impression of secrets between those two.

Mr. Quintillian was now more than ever on my mind. One day I happened to take a coffee break at the same time as Miss Parch, and I sat beside her at the counter of the short-order luncheonette in the basement of our building, and I asked her a humble question or two about our department head. To my surprise (for they had seemed peas from the same pod), she was sharply critical of him. He had wasted his life, she said. Evelyn Parch was six feet tall and was made entirely of bones, gristle, and exquisite, diaphanous skin. She was a living shame. There just wasn't enough softness for all that lovely integument of milk and honey to cover: she was like a gift-wrapped towel rack. Over her fine skin, besides, she hung knitted dresses, as if she had put a lot of thought into looking all stretched and droopy.

"Willard Quintillian," she said, "could have been president of Byron Carpets"—our firm.

Miss Parch paused and examined me, as if she expected some sort of bubble of amazement to float out of my mouth, so I said, "I simply have to take your word for it."

"He was far above my head in those days. He was Mr. Byron's favorite. Mr. Byron used to say, 'Young Quintillian is a *real* rug man. He has the right instincts. And the name is good. The i-a-n ending is very useful in a field so long dominated by Armenians, even if he isn't one himself.' You understand, Willard wasn't a boy anymore, even then." Another sharp look, as if to say, Not a boy like you.

"What happened? Where'd he get off the track?"

But Miss Parch turned away from me. She gulped her coffee and seemed sorry that she had opened up as far as she had to an untested person, one in whom Mr. Quintillian, she must have remembered, had no confidence at all.

I wondered whether I should offer to pay for Miss Parch's coffee, by way of thanks for her chary words, but as soon as I had finished I moved away and busied myself at a rack of get-well cards, picking them over until she had paid for herself.

Whereas I had at first considered Mr. Quintillian smug, finely adjusted, and set quite tight, like some old precision instrument, a metronome or a little postage scale, I now began to see many signs of loose connections, unsureness.

One morning I carried a book on trout fishing, which belonged to Charley Force, to work with me. The season was about to open upstate. I had no hope of going fishing, only of dreaming about it. I felt a deep pull in me of the countryside of my boyhood, for I was really not a city person. Mr. Quintillian's desk was centered in our cubicle, with room to walk all around it, while mine was pushed into a corner, so my back was to Mr. Quintillian and the world. I left the fishing book on the outer edge of my desk, where I could glance at its jacket and daydream.

Mr. Quintillian was performing on his adding machine crisply and feelingly, as if playing Bach two-part inventions. There came a tonic, a dominant chord, a long pause. Then, in an ice-breaking voice, he said, "I see you're an angler."

I spun around in my metal chair, startled, as if he had caught me in a mistake of figuring.

"Where do you go?" he asked.

"I used to get up north of Gloversville. In around there. Not an angler, sir. Just a bamboo pole and worms, you know."

"Best I ever knew," he said, "was the Margaree, in Nova Scotia."

"Are you," I asked with an incredulity that he could not have taken well, "are you a fisherman?"

"Used to be." A flicker, a ghost of a happy memory haunting his face. "Oh, yes," he said, shifting his papers with both hands, with a definite heartiness, his elbows too high, "I used to tie a pretty decent fly. There was one I had—blue-jay feathers—very small pale blue filoplumes that you can find in among the contour feathers on the shoulder—you know?" He paused; he seemed to be drying out rapidly. "I called it" —an adjournment now—"my Jay Walker." Rather decisively he punched the add button, and the machine whirred. I turned back to my work. I was acutely aware of the clatter of typewriters and adding machines. It seemed as if numbers and letters were flying around us like gnats.

I had a picture in my mind then of an old failure. Mr. Quintillian, who had me at his mercy, was what I wanted never to be. I felt no warmth, or even pity, only a kind of horror at this fading nonentity trying to establish a relationship with me through this blurted, fragmentary reminiscence. He was, as one could hear, a New Englander with a thin, pebbly topsoil tongue in a traprock mouth. He had come to nothing, and he was apparently willing to stake out a community of nothingness, to claim me for his void, but I didn't care to be in it.

In most people, insecurity brings out an anxiousness to please; with Mr. Quintillian it was quite the opposite. He dealt with the departmental office boys as if they were his personal servants—with an air of superiority that had a definite bite to it, for he had the unchecked power to hire and fire on our floor. More impressive was his cranky and unpredictable irritability when he spoke on the telephone with the upstairs offices, where resided the power, if there should ever be the wish, to fire *him*. He sometimes talked with higher-ups as if they were naughty children. But underneath Mr. Quintillian's avuncular snappishness I now began to detect a delicate vibration, an agitation.

How he chewed out young Scanlon one day!—an office boy who had had polio and was not your ordinary sweet polio person but instead hobbled around like an old wounded veteran of the World War, truculent and resentful, flaunting the moral elegance of his handicap: What did *you* do for your country? He had been sent off to deliver a packet of Mr. Quintillian's to the upstairs offices, and he had left it in the wrong room, and the people up there had called down, and Mr. Quintillian went after Scanlon so that you would have thought the old boy was one of those people who hated FDR precisely because he was a cripple. He apparently detested the sight of weakness or suffering of any kind. He was vicious. I had to sit there at close quarters and hear him out.

Yet I remembered, thinking back to the morning when I had caught Mr. Quintillian murmuring to Miss Tammer in our cubicle, an expression on his face then of serenity, really of something like radiance. It had been a gentle look, and a simple one: a look of simple kindness.

Mr. Quintillian had lost his wallet. Coming from the elevator at eight-twenty-two in the morning, he said someone had stolen it. He said a pickpocket had lifted it from his inner breast pocket in the elevator. The underlined implication of Mr. Quintillian's account of his loss was that a person in our company, and probably on our floor, was a pickpocket, doubtless a member of a quick-finger team, one to jostle and one to whisk. Mr. Quintillian looked knowing; he went around arresting people with stares.

Mr. Quintillian told me in our cubicle, with eyes brimming with rheum, as if his sadness at the loss had gone all thick and catarrhal and he could only weep a kind of cheese, that there had been ninety-three dollars in his wallet before its disappearance. At that announcement my heart went out to him. Money of that kind! Gone! I imagined how I would have felt at such a loss—though heaven knows I would never have been able to carry so much money around to lose. His sadness made me sad, and I realized that, after all, I did have some feeling for the old misanthrope. He was so upset. I started up a collection on our floor, to replace the stolen money, and everyone chipped in willingly, because contributing to that fund seemed to blow away the bad odor of thievery and malicious mischief that he had diffused among us as he walked gloweringly around.

When I came to the new girl, Miss Tammer, on my rounds with my hat literally in my hand, she was typing; she was in a pen with three other girls. I explained the purpose of my begging. The other three dropped in some bills and some change and tittered. Miss Tammer seemed to hesitate. She lowered her eyes and said, "Do you think he can't replace the money?" I had heard her speak.

"I know," I said. "It's kind of funny passing the tin cup for the boss. Never mind. Give a buck."

I had put in a dollar myself. That was a lot for me. I was eating for a dollar a day—ten cents for a breakfast of coffee and a doughnut, then about thirty cents for lunch and about sixty for supper at the Automat; you put the correct change in the little slots and the metal cubby door clicked open, and you pulled out whatever you had chosen, lentil soup or baked beans or beef stew—good solid food, I wasn't losing weight. I had contributed a day's food for the boss.

Miss Tammer looked at me then with a queer prim tightening of her mouth, and she said, "Okay," and she reached for her purse in the bottom drawer of her small desk, and she pulled out a dollar bill and put it in my hat.

Her eyes came up to mine again, and she leaned forward slightly, drew me down by my lapel, and spoke in a hoarse whisper against the chatter of the three machines in her cubicle, "He's a wealthy man. Didn't you know that?"

My heart began to jump rope. I don't know whether it was because Miss Tammer had confided in me, or because she had whispered to me so close that I could smell a sweet whiff of something like cinnamon on her breath, or because of what she had told me about Mr. Quintillian. Anyway, I stood there with a few dollars in my hat and my heart jouncing. It occurred to me—altogether plausibly—that Miss Tammer had been pulling my leg. I took a chance and forced out two syllables of laughter. I gulped afterward, realizing that my raucous haw-haw had been pretty crazy if she had not been kidding. I looked hopefully at her. There was a touch of amusement in her pale gray eyes, but I couldn't tell what it meant. I felt the blood climbing my cheeks. I wheeled like a drunk and fled.

Half an hour later, having gone all around the floor, I gave the money to Mr. Quintillian—about two-thirds of what he had lost, it turned out—alone in our little glass box of an office. I had no idea how he was going to react to this gift. If there was to be an explosion, as there might well be, I wanted no witnesses, because the collection had been my idea. I walked in like a brass band while he was working at his desk and just turned my hat upside down and dumped the cash in front of him.

Mr. Quintillian started counting it at once, as if he had been expecting its arrival for some time. He never looked up at me. There was a fair amount of silver, and some wise guy had tossed in a fistful of pennies. Mr. Quintillian arranged the bills in neat piles of tens, and he stacked the coins, including the pennies, in a row of cylinders of diminishing denominations.

When he was finished, he wrote on a memo pad: $63.78.

He left the money in that parade formation on his desk until lunchtime, when he made a roll of the bills and put the change in an envelope and stuffed everything in his trouser pockets, and then got up and went out. Thanks? Not a word. Not even a grunt or a hawk in his throat. I had heard his foot tapping the floor during the counting, while his thin hands fluttered and darted around the money with astonishing speed, like that of the dashing and swooping of chimney swifts on the hunt for insects in a twilight sky; perhaps that tapping had simply been a sign of his impatience with the process of counting. At any rate, it had been the only audible signal of any kind that I got from him after I spilled the money on his desk.

I had been excited by his dexterity and by his ill-concealed eagerness in handling the cash. He snapped each new bill smartly to make sure it wasn't two bills stuck together. I understand that a certain type of gambler goes short of breath with suspense when he watches a skillful dealer shuffle a deck of cards with a swift rattle and swish and two cracks of the side of the pack on the table; I'd had the same thrill seeing Mr. Quintillian count currency. Perhaps I should have been a bank teller.

More and more often, as the spring weather came on, I walked to and from the office, and for variety's sake I would take different routes. One evening, when I had decided to start downtown on Fifth Avenue, I caught a glimpse of Mr. Quintillian pushing Miss Tammer into a Number 15 double-decker bus as the door of the vehicle, like the entrapping tissue of a pitcher plant, closed and devoured the pair of them. One thing I knew: Mr. Quintillian did not live in Queens, to which buses of that number ran. I didn't know his address, but I had heard him say on the telephone one day that he lived on the Upper East Side. Nor had I found out where the new girl lived; I had, I confess, looked in all the telephone books of the metropolitan area in vain for the name Tammer. As the bus pulled away, with a sharp fart of its air brakes, I suddenly had a thought: Could she be his daughter?

I grew watchful. One day at lunchtime, having descended in the same elevator with Mr. Quintillian, following him out of the building in the most casual way, walking in the opposite direction from him for part of a block and then doubling back, I picked him out ahead, and yes, saw him meet Miss Tammer at a newsstand. Shamelessly I stalked them to the Stouffer's on Fifth. Partly to kill a few minutes and partly to have something in which to bury my face, or seem to, I went to Brentano's basement and bought the Albatross edition of *Mr. Loveday's Little Outing*, returned to the restaurant, and managed, without their having seen me, I thought, to get a table behind their backs.

What insane extravagance—to buy a book, even a thirty-cent European paperbound one—and eat at a place like Stouffer's, all in one day. I ordered only a cottage-cheese salad, but just the same! I was so absorbed in *them* that I can't even remember whether there was a charge for bread and butter.

I peeked over my book. Those two talked with animation, using enthusiastic gestures. Once in a while I saw the side of her face—glowing, mischievous.

Did she look like him? I didn't think so. It struck me then that I didn't know whether Mr. Quintillian had ever been married. Could I ask Miss Parch over coffee some morning? Or would she report to him that I was getting a shade too curious?

The time flew and their check came. Miss Tammer reached for her purse. He was fumbling in his breast pocket for the wallet he had bought to replace the stolen one. They leaned over the table; I saw his long forefinger poking above the check, as if at the ghost of an adding machine. Then each forked out paper money; she snapped open a change purse, and he fished not only in the change pouch of his right-hand jacket pocket but also in the little fob pocket at the waistband of his trousers, where, I had noticed one day at the office, he kept pennies separate from silver. They were splitting the bill right down to the last cent, and that seemed to me a strange meticulousness to be observed by a father and his daughter. And stranger yet, it struck me, for man and mistress.

One evening when we three apartment-mates were sitting in Charley's room having some beers (on Charley, as usual)—Manny and I in the overstuffed chairs and Charley on the edge of his bed—I told the other two how mystified I was about Mr. Quintillian and Miss Tammer. Charley became excited. He wanted me to introduce him to Miss Tammer, said he'd get to the bottom of the thing in two shakes. I said I couldn't possibly do that; I didn't know her well enough. Then Charley began to have great fun guessing. She was the old bugger's niece, had been shipped up to the city by Mr. Q's elder sister, who had always hated him. No, she was his bastard child by what was that dried-up head typist's name—Miss Perch? Maybe she was working him for dough. Maybe she was a gold digger who liked the digging more than the gold, so she had staked herself out on a really hardpan case. Nope. It was just an innocent relationship, she was touched by him, sorry for him, wanted to bring him out of himself, so she began inveigling him out on the town—entertainments that would appeal to a tightwad—"You know, Doug, the kinds of things *you*'d do with a girl on a date, the big room with all the armor in it at the Metropolitan, a twenty-cent ride up Riverside Drive on the open top of a double-decker bus"—and pretty soon they're in love—it's possible, you know, some girls want their fathers back.

"Oh, no!" he then said. "I *know* what it is. This old guy is bitter because promises made to him years ago haven't been kept. He handles the money in your department, right? He has this strongbox, right? For ages now, he's been diddling Byron Carpets, just a little bit at a time, I mean he's a small-change kind of swindler. But these itty-bitty peculations add up, you know. They add up. And somehow this dame finds out, right? She gets on his soft side, puts on an extra dab of perfume, know what I mean? Then, wham, on the upper deck of a bus to Queens she tells him she knows, and she strings him out with a nasty little run of blackmail."

I was suddenly furious. "What balls," I said to Charley. "You're really disgusting." I threw my empty beer bottle in his wastebasket and walked out to the other room.

Charley called after me, "Aha, Douglas old sport. I get it why you don't want to introduce her to me."

It came to me the next day that the reason I had been so

upset by Charley's game of guessing was that each of his speculations seemed to me, turn by turn, so possible, so believable—and perhaps especially the last of them. Perhaps a deeper reason I'd been angry was that the guessing game was so much fun. I could play it, too. I became convinced that Miss Tammer had some sort of hold on poor Quintillian. Could she have found among the secret innermost furnishings of his heart, and threatened to expose, some antique New England love seat where lust and avarice sat guiltily side by side? I began to think Miss Tammer must be a tough number, and I began to feel sorry for Mr. Quintillian.

In the next few days I had no chance to see them together, and then there came an upheaval at Byron Carpets that turned everything upside down.

Even I had been noticing for some time that the numbers that crept across the desks of our department had been bad. People out there just couldn't afford rugs. We all knew that upstairs Mr. Byron was worried. One day a time-study man prowled around our floor, as discreet and menacing as an FBI agent. There were rumors of "some changes." Mr. Quintillian was called upstairs several times; he returned pale and tight-lipped. Then one day the bolt landed—a memorandum, circulated to everyone in the whole company, even the office boys. The memo—signed with flourishes and curlicues by Chester Byron, Jr., President—announced to us that Ernst & Callaghan, management consultants, were coming in "to bring us up to date in all respects."

An office boy dropped one copy of the document on Mr. Quintillian's desk and another on mine at almost the same moment. As I read mine, I thought I heard Mr. Quintillian humming a tune. I did not dare turn my head. It was only much later, when I had gone home that evening, that I realized what I had heard was moaning. Yet afterward, during the rest of the day, Mr. Quintillian was not unusually bad-tempered;

if anything, I would have said he was rather more civil to me than usual. But those sounds he had made, those musical utterances, in a chest or belly tone like that of a tenor in the lowest reaches of his range at the end of a tragic aria, haunted me all afternoon.

In a few days there came from upstairs an avalanche of paper. Form after modernizing form flopped onto our desks. A species of non-language crawled across each of these.

A firm pen or pencil should be used, please bear down on these six part inner carbon dupes. Conform entries to previously described sets. New sets are budgetarily non-transferable. For any salary fraction whose source is changing enter new account number (four digits dash two digits dash five digits) in the column marked "Acct numb or descr of source funds." If the account number is unavailable, describe the future source (e.g., "Expediting and Rationalization Department—applied for"; see note 4 in "General Instructions" for continuation numbers). Then record the dollar and cent figure. Be careful to columnarize properly the type source for either recommended or spent dollars. . . .

Next there landed on the desks of our department sets of huge new triple-entry ledgers, each with a long mimeographed text of instructions, composed in that same pseudolanguage. I expected an outburst in our cubicle. Quite the contrary. Never had Mr. Quintillian been so accommodating, so soft-spoken. That afternoon I actually saw him giving Scanlon, the office boy who'd had polio, an encouraging pat on the shoulder. He told me my work was getting a little better. At Stouffer's a couple of days later, peering cautiously over a Tauchnitz paperback of *Nostromo*, I thought I saw him hold up a forbidding hand when Miss Tammer picked up her purse to pay for her own lunch. Of course I could construe such a gesture now

with any of several meanings, but it did seem part of a definite
pattern of softening in Mr. Quintillian.

After lunchtime that Friday, just as Mr. Quintillian was
unlocking his strongbox to start counting out our pay, I heard
Scanlon's uneven clip-clop coming along the passageway and
into our cubicle.

"Hello, son," Mr. Quintillian said perfectly pleasantly.
"What have you got for me?"

"Envelope from His Nibs," Scanlon said.

I hadn't turned around. Mr. Quintillian must have taken
the envelope from Scanlon's outreached hand. I heard a murmur
of thanks. I heard paper tearing. Then silence for a few moments. Then, very softly, some low notes of that awful aria I
had heard once before. Then I heard a squeal of Mr. Quintillian's swivel chair, and his footsteps as he left the office.

Now I turned around, and I saw that Mr. Quintillian had
taken his topcoat and hat from the rack in the corner. On his
desktop next to his huge adding machine I saw a torn envelope
and, held down by his celluloid eyeshade, what appeared to
be the single sheet of a letter. And also, to one side, the
strongbox with its top wide open.

I didn't know what to do. For a long time I just sat there
waiting. I supposed Mr. Quintillian must have felt a desperate
need to go out for a cup of coffee, or perhaps the letter had
peremptorily ordered him out on some urgent errand. But it
was utterly unlike him to leave the strongbox, with so much
cash in it that I trembled to think of it, open on his desk. I
sat staring at the figures I had been working on. I have no
idea how much time passed—perhaps an hour, perhaps two
—before I stood up with a thumping heart, stepped to Mr.
Quintillian's desk, peered first at all the money neatly stacked
in denominations in compartments in the strongbox, and then
lifted off the eyeshade and turned the typed page around and
read it.

Mr. Quintillian

TO: All Department Heads
FROM: Chester Byron, Jr., President

You will be pleased, I am sure, to know that on advice of Ernst & Callaghan, the weekly pay of all employees of Byron Carpets will henceforth be issued by check. I am certain that all of you will be immensely relieved not to have the responsibility of the cash transactions with which we have burdened you for so many years. Check-writing machines were installed here on the ninth floor during the past week, and the first paychecks will be distributed by the messenger desk on each floor later this afternoon. With thanks as always for your loyal and trustworthy service.

I closed the strongbox and twirled its dial, as I had seen Mr. Quintillian do, to lock it. Then I sat down at my desk and, staring again at the figures I had been working on, I wondered for a long time what to do. At a little after four, I heard the creak of the door from the elevator bank swinging open, and after that the squishing sound of Mr. Quintillian's rubber heels on the polished tiles of the passageway—but there was something wrong with the rhythm of the squishes. He came banking around the barrier with his coat flapping like an alighting gull's wings. And yes, here he came, this old geezer, weaving like a brain-busted pug on the verge of a TKO. He crashed into his chair and sat there humming that awful sound. An odor of alcohol quickly filled our cubicle, as rank as the afterburn of a car's exhaust in a garage when the engine has been turned off.

I waited a discreet few moments and then got up and went along to Miss Tammer's compartment, and I asked her if I might speak to her out in the passageway for a moment. I whispered to her that Mr. Q was drunk. She took a step toward our cubicle, but I told her she had better get her hat and purse. She did that, and we went along to the stall at the end of the passageway.

Mr. Quintillian still had his hat and coat on. She said to him in a low voice, "We're going to go home now, Willard."

He looked up at her and, seeming not to recognize her, smiled and nodded. Miss Tammer and I helped him stand up, and with one of us on each side of him we managed to get him out to the bank of elevators without anyone from the office having seen us.

In the street I did not hesitate for a moment to raise my arm for a taxi. When one pulled over, we bundled Mr. Quintillian in, and I went around to the far door, so he would be seated in the middle. Miss Tammer gave an address on East Ninetieth Street. The driver chose to go up Park Avenue. As my shoulder bounced against the limp figure of the old man, I felt a surge of revulsion and anger. That night, in my room, I realized that these feelings, directed at Mr. Quintillian and partly even at Miss Tammer, probably stemmed from the disastrous news I was reading, block after endless block, on the cab's meter, because it would be a matter of course that I would have to pay the fare. It would also come to me that night, though, that there may have been some pity mixed in with my resentment, as, breathing the fumes of Mr. Quintillian's boozing, I had dimly begun to know what must have blocked his rise, years ago, to the top of Byron Carpets.

Our goal turned out to be a brownstone walk-up, not much different from the one I lived in. We had to pause often on the way to the fourth floor. In its hallway Miss Tammer knew exactly what to do. She unbuttoned Mr. Quintillian's topcoat, reached her hand into his left trouser pocket, drew out his keys, and unlocked the door. And we teetered in.

I was shocked, looking around at our boss's digs—shaken by a question at the edge of my mind. Could such a hole as this be in *my* future? It was a one-room affair, with a tiny alcove as a kitchenette. There was a white-painted cast-iron bedstead with floral designs at the tops of the spindles; two straight wooden chairs; a round table with a green felt cloth thrown over it; a chiffonier with nothing on it but a pair of brass-backed military hairbrushes, the bristles of one stuck into those of the other. On the round table there were two photographs, a pair of dark eyes in one and a bald head with a bump on it in the other shouting that these must have been Mr. Q's parents.

We got Mr. Quintillian's hat and topcoat off and balanced him in a seated position on the edge of his bed. Miss Tammer, starting to take off his jacket, turned to me and firmly said, "I can manage now."

I was taken aback by her level look and by the implications of this announcement, since she was obviously going to have to undress him and tuck him in. Mumbling absurd thanks for her help, I left. I realized, the moment the outer street door clicked shut behind me, that I would have no way of reaching Miss Tammer over the weekend to find out how things had gone.

On Monday morning I got to the office as usual between eight and eight-fifteen. Mr. Quintillian arrived soon after me. He said good morning cheerfully. A quick sidelong glance at his eyes brought to my mind a vivid memory of the piercing and defiant glare of a trout I had once caught with a worm and a bamboo pole in the stream near Gloversville—a look to say, I have swum a thousand miles; the worm that caught me was delicious. As if nothing had changed, he lifted the locked cash box off his desk and put it in its usual place in a corner. Then he sat down, donned and adjusted his eyeshade, and went right to work on some figures.

I had a problem on my hands. Returning to the office on Friday afternoon, after the trip to Ninetieth Street, I had found my paycheck on my desk and Mr. Quintillian's on his. Mine was made out wrong—fifty cents short of my due. Mr. Quintillian's desk drawers were all locked, so I had placed his check for safekeeping in one of mine. I was apprehensive now about how he might take my handing his wages over to him—a check issued upstairs—in what would surely be a humiliating reversal of roles, since he had always paid me off in cash. Not once, by the way, with an error of so much as a penny. The worst of it was that he would be bound to assume that I had noticed the amount embossed by the check-writing machine in bold barred blue figures on his check. I had noticed, all right. Yes, I had taken the trouble to notice. I had had to look at the figure twice. I could not believe how little our department head, this "real rug man," this ruin with a gift for figures, was being paid after all the years.

Suddenly, as I sat there unsure what to do about the check, I felt a wave of anger at those barbarians of "efficiency," Ernst & Callaghan, breaking in on the settled habits of our floor with their meddlesome new procedures, their memos and machines, and their half-dollar mistakes. The anger made me reckless. I pulled Mr. Quintillian's check from my drawer, wheeled in my chair without standing, and leaned over to slide the check toward him.

I said, "Found it on your desk Friday. Thought it ought to be in a drawer." I turned back to my work.

I heard a quiet voice say, "Thank you, Douglas."

He had never before used my first name.

Nothing would do after that but a talk with Miss Tammer. It took me two weeks to get up my courage to approach her. Not being sure what her relationship with Mr. Quintillian amounted to, I felt that I had to be very careful. Bad enough to be rebuffed; worse to have her tell him behind my back that I was trying some funny business.

Making a date turned out to be ridiculously simple. I was

elaborate and she was not. I took a late lunch one day and afterward called her at the office from a pay telephone booth in a drugstore. I blurted out my question. Airily and easily she said yes.

We met on a fine night in May. I had made severely cautious plans—asked her to meet me at a bar on Second Avenue, way uptown, north of Yorkville, in what she might have thought of as a marginal district. It was a dark place with a high ceiling made of squares of tin embossed with wreaths and roses; the noises of the place reverberated from the stamped tin, seemed even amplified by it. A jukebox thumped and whined. Some workmen laughed and argued around a long, narrow slab, along which they slid heavy metal disks about the size of hockey pucks to knock down electrically operated tenpins; shooting, the men screwed up their faces and chewed their tongues, as if they were great sculptors at work or third-graders trying to memorize multiplication tables. The whole time we were there, one of the customers at the bar shouted what seemed to be threats in some guttural foreign language, possibly Gaelic; perhaps he was announcing the end of the world. A drunken woman on one of the bar stools held on a leash of wrapping twine a mongrel dog, which put its head back and howled from time to time. Altogether, the atmosphere of the place rattled me, just when I wanted to be at my smoothest and be able to talk in confidential tones.

Because I had said on the phone that we wouldn't be doing anything fancy, Miss Tammer was wearing a sweater and skirt and some of those big fake pearls that pop into each other— which, along with her crownlike braid and her wax-paper skin, were very becoming, I thought. Like a fool I had dressed in a dark blue suit, and it embarrassed me that Miss Tammer would notice how glaringly we stuck out among the working people in the place.

I went to the bar, where somber men sat silent behind shots of rye with beer chasers, and I ordered a couple of martinis.

The barman, who was also, I guess, the owner, winked at me, as if to say, French-type behavior calls for French-type drinks, huh? And he mixed equal parts of gin and vermouth and poured them into wineglasses and charged me eighty cents for the pair. I am not the kind of person who sends things back to be done over again, and I carried the drinks to our booth, spilling a few drops as I went.

We sipped and sipped in silence. Then abruptly I said, "About Mr. Quintillian's money."

"*What?*" She sounded testy. I regretted having plunged in so rashly on what I wanted to know.

"That day, um, he lost his wallet," I said. "When I was taking up a collection. You told me—you told me—that he's rich."

She laughed, but it was an awful laugh, the kind one coughs out to cover one's confusion over an awkwardness that has caused a companion to stub his toe or bump into a lamp post. But then she said, "I thought you asked me out because you were interested in *me*."

This coyness—or maybe it was mockery—rubbed the wrong way. I said, "I need to know."

"What business is it of yours?"

"He's changed."

Suddenly her eyes were brimming with tears. "I didn't like your taking up a collection. I thought it was insulting. I thought you were making fun of him."

"You were making fun of *me*. He can't be rich. God, I've seen what they pay him."

"How do you mean, 'changed'?"

"He's been so good to me in the last few days. He's suddenly Mr. Sunshine. Is it you who have made him so ridiculously happy?"

Now this tough number really was crying. "When do you think you saw this begin—this—this cheerfulness?"

"Is it money? I want to know, Miss Tammer. The way these

efficiency fiends are wrecking our business. Are they buying him off?"

"Tell me when you noticed," she said.

"After we took him home that day. But really in a big way starting last Monday. He's so considerate it makes me sick. He's not himself."

She took out a Kleenex and blew her nose. Then, obviously trying to get herself in hand, she seemed to be studying her glass. She was very pale. Finally, twirling the stem of the glass, and still staring at it, she said, "Monday was the day they let him go. Fired him. After thirty-four years, they gave him two weeks' notice."

I felt as if she'd slapped me. "Jesus God, why couldn't he be angry?"

"It's not me. You have to know him. He's a saintly person. He told me a month ago that this was going to happen. He said we have to face things, the world is changing."

My own anger suddenly floated free. I found that I was wildly angry at my roommate Charley Force because he would have known how to carry on through a ruined evening with such an attractive girl. Yet I hated her, too. How disgusting, to try to make a saint of that pathetic man. How could she say so breezily that she thought I'd asked her out because I liked her? Face things? I raged at a world that could change so easily right in front of my eyes. And then I realized that my anger was iced with fear. Face things? What kind of future was I supposed to face now, at Byron Carpets, or anywhere? The moment that question began to hover in my mind I pushed it aside, only to sense that my anxiety had abruptly swerved toward the hour at hand. How was I going to get Miss Tammer home? I could hardly walk her all the way down to Fifty-seventh Street and dump her on a Number 15 bus. A taxi, its meter racing, all the way to Queens?

I think she must have seen perspiration on my forehead.

Like a mind reader, knowing that our evening had so soon come to an end, she put her hand on mine and said, "Don't worry about me, Douglas." My first name again. It came to me that I didn't even know hers. "I'm going to Ninetieth Street," she said. "It's only a couple of blocks from here. We can walk."

The Terrorist

Sometimes, in moments of high energy like this one, he sees himself as a character in a comic strip. This fragments his action. Jerks him through life. The strip is called *The Iron Guerrilla*. It has four panels. It is on the right-hand side of the funnies page, as he sees it, sandwiched between *Blondie* and *Rip Kirby*, and butted end-to-end with *Dick Tracy* on the inner tier of strips.

FIRST PANEL

In the first panel of today's strip, he is running from left to right. He *is* running, but as he sees himself in this piece of the action, he is frozen in place in a drawing. A certain distortion—a pulling downward of his extended left leg and a pulling out rearward of his right leg—shows speed. His being arrested in mid-race in newsprint like this has psychological verity: he is running but he can't move. He sees himself wearing what he *is* wearing as he runs: a little Gorky cap with a patent-leather visor, denim jacket, jeans, desert boots—the right one of which has dirty adhesive tape wound round and round the forefoot. No color, of course; the jeans aren't blue;

the strip is in black-and-white. This is like a passage in a
dream. The iron guerrilla dreams in black-and-white. His
straight hair would be shoulder-length, but now with his
motion it flies out behind in free waves. Wow, that hair has
been shampooed. Followers of the strip, as he would say, know
that other characters in it sometimes refer to him as The Kleen
Krazy. He is shaven. What the fuck—or fugg, as The Kleen
Krazy prefers to put it—kind of an iron guerrilla is it who
has no beard?

Looking closer at the rest of the panel, one sees a street sign:
MEETINGHOUSE LANE. This has to be Boston. Why does the
strip buff know that? Well, what other for-real city with its
head put together would have a street sign reading MEETING-
HOUSE LANE? Anyone who knows Boston knows there are
actually *four* Meetinghouse Lanes, all in the same downtown
area. So there we are. The iron guerrilla is passing the inter-
section of HIGGINSON STREET. To the right of the panel, in
the direction in which he is running, is the corner of a building,
which any proper Bostonian would recognize as the new main
branch of the First Transcendental Bank & Trust Company.
Trust is what the iron guerrilla wants to blow up. Yes, he
runs with both hands in front of him, they are black, he is
wearing rubber gloves. In his left hand is his walkie-talkie
radio. Its antenna has a fifty-nine-inch hard-on. This is a
Peerless 21-112 one-watt one-channel talk box with a solid-
state circuit and extrasensitive RF amplifier stage to really pull
in the signals. Looking at himself in the panel, he can see that
his thumb is wrapped around the box and so is not on the
PRESS-TO-TALK button. Indeed, out of the tiny aluminum
speaker with its sparkling triangulations comes a speech balloon. In it these words are printed (he hears them as he runs
and also sees them in the panel in his head): THIS IS LOGO
ONE. ALL CLEAR. KEEP COMING. This whole schmear is a kind
of discontinuous comic-strip dream game. In his right hand

is the explosive device. This is a wicked-pissa little package. Six half-sticks of dyna bundled into fasces and, at the end, a $29.95 Superclox shock-resistant antimagnetic unbreakable-mainspring (something is going to break it yeah man) alarm clock, face out and wired, it must be presumed, to a detonator, which cannot be seen in the small scale of the bomb in this panel. Beautiful compact infernal machine in his right hand as he runs toward the bank.

SECOND PANEL

Here the iron guerrilla is seen leaning forward near the flap-mouthed metal slot marked NITE DEPOSIT BOX on the front of the bank, next to the main entrance. One can assume that there has been action since the first panel—more running, thumb pressure on the TALK button of the Raider, a four-syllable report, OKAY SO FAR, and other such fantastic doings. But the beauty part of seeing life as a comic strip is just this. If life looks like anything to your average everyday male or female person, it looks like a series of discrete, zapped instants. Dullness, click, dullness, click, dullness dullness, click, dullness, click. A lot of the time it is just dullness dullness dullness dullness dullness. In his appreciation of the comic-strip vision of life, however, the iron guerrilla has in mind high-energy passages like the present one, in which dullness is reduced to tolerable time periods, or panels.

In following a panoramic strip, as any comics addict knows, it is obligatory to see the main character in a close-up. The iron guerrilla's face is in profile. He is a looker. Somewhat the Steve McQueen type, but darker. Macho jaw, poet's eyes. At the present time he has a hyped expression. Face of the last two strides of a sixty-yard dash, this man is ahead, he is going to win, he sees the tape. He is having a radical high, he is stoned on the fitness of what he is doing. There is a fine wrinkle of pathos stretching from near his right nostril down to the near right corner of his mouth, which suggests an occasional dark sneaky suspicion in The Kleen Krazy's mind that he is, or may be, a sad-ass. Mostly, though, the face is lit up with a really creamy euphoria: this is the interface with the Enemy.

Now we can also see another face, that of the clock on the bomb. It reads six-twenty-two. Your faithful follower of this particular strip knows this means ante meridiem. Even an iron guerrilla with a clean-shaven chin doesn't go around doing bombs at six-twenty-two in the evening, when the People's metabolism is revved up and they are milling in the streets. Nowhere in the first two panels has there been any clue about what day of the week it is, but again, any *Iron Guerrilla* freak knows it has to be Sunday morning to do a bomb on a bank. You don't want any fragging here; it is the institution, not its exploited personnel, that you want to prang. Since it is this light at this hour, it has to be something like springtime at Boston's latitude, which, according to The Kleen Krazy, ought to be 42°20' N. In fact, the dateline of the paper at the top of the funnies page tells the reader that it is April 1, 1969. It is April Fools' Day. A day for pranks—or, in other words, prangs. The guerrilla in this early-morning-in-Beantown panel is stuffing the infernal machine in the NITE DEPOSIT BOX. This is the first joke of the strip. A four-panel comic strip needs two laughs: a little one to set up the big one, and then the big one to justify all this artwork. This panel has the first joke. It is the anticipatory boffo. *The guerrilla is making a big deposit in the piggy bank.* Above The Kleen Krazy's head as he slips the business to the deposit-twat is a thought balloon. What indicates that this is a thought balloon rather than a speech balloon, of course, is that instead of the usual pointed lead-out to the balloon from the character's head, there is a series of small bubblelike circles drifting away from his head toward the main balloon. In the thought balloon are printed the words of the iron guerrilla's thought at this moment: IT IS HYPO-CRITICAL TO BE AGAINST VIOLENCE PER SE. WE TEND TO BE AGAINST VIOLENCE ONLY WHEN ITS USE RUNS COUNTER TO OUR PERCEIVED VALUES. THIS IS A GOOD BOMB. Har-de-har. The device just fits the deposit slot. It has obviously been designed to fit this very slot. The iron guerrilla leans forward. On his face is this look of political orgasm. The good bomb is going into the bad bank.

THIRD PANEL

This is where the *big* joke comes. At the center of the panel are three letters. Each one is as tall as Kareem going up for a tip-off. P! . . . O! . . . W! A subsidiary joke to the panel's hyperjoke is that these letters might stand for Prisoner of War. Radiating around from these letters is a representation of your average big-time Alamogordo megaton bust-out. Whew, it is a funky bang. Jagged lines. Bold. Electric. White space at the center denoting great thermal jism and vitality. Ringed about above this chrysanthemum of energy are bits and pieces of social history. Chunks of masonry and safe-deposit boxes flying outward, dollar bills, small change, government bonds, stock certificates, South African investments, contracts to jell napalm, letters to the Rockefellers, savings-bank passbooks of Nguyen Cao Ky and Ferdinand Marcos and Chiang Kai-shek's oldest son. Chilean copper-mine shares. Pentagon escrow ac-counts, and various other kinds of triple-entry shit—or shite, as The Kleen Krazy would have it. Beautiful. In the lower left-hand corner of the panel there can be seen just the jeaned leg of a man running away. On the foot is a desert boot wrapped around with dirty adhesive tape. Because, except for this leg, the iron guerrilla has made an exit from this panel, he cannot see what has happened behind him when the shite hit the fan. He can only imagine it. But then the whole strip is in his imagination. He *is* running away.

In the final panel he is still running. We cannot see a street sign, but he appears to have turned a corner because we now see him from the rear. He is running away from the surface of the page. Again his haste is frozen. (We recall that the entire strip is in his head. Actually running, he is psyched into immobility.) His back is straight. The right foot, the one we have seen marked with adhesive tape, is extended forward and is hidden by his left leg or his torso—the view is slightly from above; the left foot, reaching back toward the page level and the imaginary reader's eye, is turned somewhat in and is on a line with his right buttock. This suggests a touch of bowleggedness, which in turn insinuates in the viewer's mind a rush of sympathy for one who really does appear to be a sad-ass on the run. The washed hair is fixed in mid-bounce. Because this is a rear view, we of course cannot see the iron guerrilla's face, but we have one clue to its expression. There is a balloon up to the right of the fleeing Krazy's head. Bubbles float between the head and the balloon. This is the magic of a comic strip. We are given insight into the character's mental processes without hearing a single word or seeing a facial change of any kind. In the balloon are these words: JEEZUS, THAT WAS TOO CLOSE! DID SOME "FRIEND" TAMPER WITH THE TIMER? IM GETTING PARANOID AS FUGG. The comic-strip buff will translate this into a simpler thought: Am *I* the fool on this first of April, 1969?

In the distance, beyond and to the left of the running iron guerrilla, at the corner of the next block, we see a female figure. We can tell it is a woman by the curving lines in the

denim shirt that could not possibly be pockets. Also there is
something about the hips. Otherwise—jeans, shirt, Gorky
cap, hair—the figure might be interchangeable with that of
the main character. This woman is in a posture of extreme
elation. Obviously she has heard the beautiful big bang. She
has her arms raised in a V-for-Victory sign (in one hand is a
walkie-talkie—ah! was she guerrilla's lookout, possibly Logo
One?)—precisely the gesture—this is *incredible*—precisely the
gesture the strip buff would often have seen Nixon making
on the tube. As he stepped out of the plane onto the platform
of the landing stairway. Out of a car. In front of a crowd.
With his shoulders hunched up as only an ex-third-stringer
on the Whittier College football team would hunch. The
shoulders of this woman have *this same hunch*. How come an
urban guerrilla is mimicking the Total Nix? This anomaly can
only be attributed to the phenomenon known as transcultural
media pollution—like an anthropologist exploring deepest
bush in Zaire comes across a native tyke in a *Yellow Submarine*
T-shirt. These things happen.

And so this is the end of today's strip. The hook. We have
had a glimpse of the Mysterious Woman. The iron-guerrilla
buff will find it hard to wait for tomorrow's panels. Here in
the trashed-bank payoff panel the central character is running
away from the imaginary reader (but because drawn, remember, he is frozen—as if, one might guess, with a terrorist's
terror, or it may even be that self-doubt paralyzes him). He
is running toward a female "accomplice." Thinking suspicious
thoughts. The reader is allowed to have thoughts, too. Is
paranoia paranoia when there probably has been and surely
will be real danger? Is the Mysterious Woman an undercover
agent of the FBI? Was her mimicking of the Nix shrug un-
conscious transcultural media pollution, after all, or was it
deliberate—a sign to the knowing reader? And followers of
the strip will long have been wondering: Who really *is* the

iron guerrilla? Is he a genuine folk hero? Or is he a Harvard sophomore? What Calvinist chromosomes make him so kleen that he cannot utter a straightforward oath? Are fugg and shite aspects of idealism? Is the sole of his right shoe really loose or did he put the adhesive tape around it just to make his mother angry? Now that we think of it, is the FBI agent perhaps a senior at Radcliffe (later also to be known as "Harvard")? On a deeper level of significance, has Trust been pranged? Has History swerved in Her course? Has the iron guerrilla struck a significant blow against defoliation in Southeast Asia? Are the Rockefellers trembling in their boots? Will we have peace in our time? As all good comic-strip loyalists must do, we must take a look tomorrow. And the next day. And the next day.

Affinities

Bailiff Esposito unlocked the door from the jail, and Clerk Cherevoy went through to get the night list and copies of police reports and prior records. This always took time; there were rituals of deploring to be got through with the duty lieutenant. Joel Avered sat down in the jury box to wait.

During arraignment sessions, Joel had come to think of the jury box as his office. There was no assigned place for bondsmen in the Pit—as everyone referred to the ancient courtroom— and sometimes he felt like an extra thumb, especially first thing in the morning. Still, he was pleased with himself for being on hand so early. There were six bondsmen in the city, and he could honestly say that none worked at the job as hard as he. Three were Catholics, two were Jews, and he was the surprise White Anglo-Saxon Protestant entry. Joel took some ragging, but he was not ashamed to talk about, and adhere to, the celebrated work ethic of his persuasion. Sarah often complained, when his phone rang at three o'clock in the morning and he would arise groaning and dress groaning and drive all the way into town to get a client out of jail, that being married to him was like being married to a doctor. Joel liked that. He hated to see young people locked up, especially for the first time. An unhealthy environment. All those who were

obliged to appear in court knew that there was one bail bondsman who would take the trouble to get a postponement and
chase them down if they forgot to show up for trial, so they
wouldn't have to forfeit their bond. Joel Avered was famous
in the part of Treehampstead known as "the Valley." He could
walk there alone at night, along the worst streets, Congress
Avenue, Framwell, Cahoon—"Hey Mist' Aved, who you
lookin' for?" He had learned not to let himself be invited into
bars; there were too many poor people who wanted to buy Joel
Avered a drink.

Alexander Cherevoy came back from the lockup carrying
his sheaf of papers. With his mouth gathered into a bud
of self-importance, he walked right past the jury box. Joel
knew enough not to make a move. The clerk went to his
desk and got out some file folders, and he began typing
names on gummed labels, licking the labels with a wide,
whitish tongue, and sticking them on the tabs of the folders;
afterward he inserted police reports and prior-record sheets
into the appropriate folders. Joel knew just how long it would
take before the clerk would break off this work and call out,
"Oh jeez, Avered, you wanted to see the list. Sorry, fella.
Pick up."

At this summons, Joel went to the clerk's desk, took the
sheet of onion-skin paper from the clerk's hand, and carried
it back to the jury box.

This morning there were seven Found Intoxicateds, two
Motor Vehicles bad enough for jail arrest, one Soliciting, two
Breaking & Enterings with Larceny, three Possessions, a Wel-
fare Fraud, a Failure to Support, and several Disorderlies.
A thin morning, unless the Larcenies turned out to be plums;
it would depend on what had been taken.

He went down the list again, reading the particulars, and
this time one of the items jumped out at him. He had never
seen such a charge before.

Samson Honniger, B & E/grand larc, theft of dog.

The word "dog" jolted Joel. His folk memory had long since endowed this room, which was two stories high and had a temple-like austerity, with hints of Judgment Day. The jury box consisted of a brace of pews ransacked, he would have sworn, from some old Congregational church. The flaking ceiling far overhead was supported by half a dozen slender steel stanchions like the soaring pillars of a cathedral. The judge's bench was to Joel's right, a raised wooden cockpit which resembled a pulpit. Up the wall behind him were tall, narrow sash windows with Gothic peaks; they could be thought of as stained-glass windows, for their lights were tinted with grime that must have been ancient as sin in the polluted days and nights of the Oak City. It had always seemed to Joel that human souls were in transaction here, and the sudden involvement of an animal—would *its* soul be in the balance, too?—was somehow disturbing.

Joel took the list back to the clerk's desk. He had to stand and wait, because the clerk and the bailiff were chatting. Alexander Cherevoy was tall, wore gray suits, and had the sallow complexion and fine wrinkles of some endocrinal imbalance; Sal Esposito was short and swarthy, wore blue suits with an enameled American flag in the buttonhole, and was a living sculpture in pasta. Between them, Joel had long ago observed, these two set the tone of the Pit. Judges, prosecutors, public defenders, bondsmen, probation officers, bail commissioners—all of them came and went, but Cherevoy and Esposito were eternal. They were, Joel had once thought, like the figures he had seen in pictures of fountains in Rome—grand, dramatic, watery, ferocious. The tone they maintained was one of disapproval. You could read in their faces that in Fifth Circuit Court things were getting worse from day to day, and even from hour to hour. The clerk laughed more than the bailiff did, but the laughter of both seemed scornful to

Joel. Both were courteous to defendants, and toward black culprits their manners were always especially impeccable, but their courtesy had in it the distance from this world of galaxies of ice and fire. Any kind word they spoke to any defendant less than twenty-five years old, black or white, rang with the hollow sound of the rule of law. Bestowing on Joel the same courtesy they showed to criminals, they drew him now into their little chat.

Alexander Cherevoy's passion was the accumulation of trophies received from what seemed to be a horde of postcard-exchangers all over the world, people who networked collectors' addresses and sent cards to total strangers in foreign countries expecting due return. He had been asking Sal Esposito to translate one he had received the day before, and now he passed it to Joel without a word. It showed a black-and-white picture of the Hotel Sphinx in Cairo. On the other side it had an ornate Egyptian stamp, was addressed to Onorevole Giudice Alessandro Cherevoy, in care of the courthouse, and bore this message: *"Ecco il più squisito albergo egiziano. La mia cugina Maria Francesca Sottotavole m'ha mandato da Livorno il Suo indirizzo. Sia gentilissimo, Onorevole Giudice Cherevoy, e mi manda per posta una bella carta postale da Treehampstead, Connecticut. Buona fortuna e mille grazie."* The signature was so weedy with flourishes as to be almost illegible, but the return address of this Italian devotee of collectibles living in a Cairo suburb was meticulously printed.

" *'Giudice,'* " Joel said. "Doesn't that mean 'Judge'?"

"Yeah," Sal Esposito said. "This fellow went and gave Alex a promotion."

Cherevoy asked (rather angrily, it seemed to Joel), "Where'd you learn Italian?"

Joel felt apologetic. "So many of my clients . . . Just a smattering." He thought it best to change the subject. "I was wondering, could I see the report on Honniger—the Honniger on this list?"

Cherevoy made a pair of pliers of his right thumb and forefinger and snatched the card away from Joel. "Come *on*, Avered. You know I'm not allowed to show you the papers beforehand. What's the matter with you this morning?"

Joel retired to his "office." A few minutes later, when the bailiff had left the Pit on some errand, the clerk stepped over to Joel and handed him the Honniger report. "You should know by now," Cherevoy said, "not to ask special favors in front of other people."

Joel was astonished by this sudden kindness, and he wondered whether his having known the Italian word for "judge" and so having cast a bright light on the postal promotion may have marked a slight turning point in Alex Cherevoy's attitude toward him. He thanked him for the favor. Then he read the report. It merely said:

Complainant Geoffrey Alford called headquarters at 11:43 p.m. giving name and address of perpetrator. Officer Onofrio, Car 20, reported from perpetrator's premises that the stolen article (dog, valued by complainant at five hundred dollars) was in perpetrator's possession. Perpetrator arrested. Dog returned to complainant. Confirmation from complainant that he wished to press charges.

That was all. Joel returned the paper to the clerk, who had stood by waiting for it. "Odd case," Joel said.

"Surprised?" the clerk said. "Where you been all your life? They're *all* oddballs, from the word go. Every damn one of them."

In truth it might be said that they were. Here they came for arraignment, one by one. Behind Joel's left shoulder was the door from the jail, through which the accused were led blinking into the bright light of the big room. Sometimes, in his easier moods, Joel thought of the Pit not as a tainted place of worship but as a theater. Across the room from where he sat was a low wooden fence with a clicking gate at the center, presided over by Sal Esposito, the bailiff, and beyond that were several rows of folding chairs for families and onlookers —the audience. At the heart of the court was a worn patch of floorboards—planks of a stage on which, as it seemed to Joel, farce and satire and burlesque and vaudeville routines wearily stretched themselves out day after day, each successive act reaching hopelessly for the unattainable relief that tragedy would have given.

Here came the heavies. What faces!—ravaged, jaunty, dazed, defiant, disenchanted, raging, resigned. A man in his forties ("found intox," on the list), whom Joel had seen here often before, clutching in his arms a stuffed cloth tiger nearly as tall as he, his constant companion and only comfort. Three weedlike, red-eyed minors in blue jeans—said to have been breakers and enterers. A natty type, accused of failure to support his wife and babies, in a whipcord bush jacket and knickers and smartly polished leather puttees. A woman booked as a whore, with a pokey-soiled wig and a hacking cough, badly in need of night's more merciful light. An empty-faced teenager, held for possession of a controlled substance, with his mother, who was obviously played out to the very end of her kitchen string, on hand to stand up with him. . . .

Late in the morning Clerk Cherevoy stood and in tones of doom called out, "Case of Samson Honniger."

The duty policeman that morning was Tony Netto, whom Joel considered far and away the best of the city's cops. He called all the young punks "dearie," and he applied handcuffs as if he were a hairdresser patting curls. Joel had one day reflected that the female principle lodged in the male breast

made for the purest kind of justice. There was no officer so
naturally in tune with the Bill of Rights as Nelly Netto, as
his colleagues called him, and there was none so brave. No
Treehampstead policeman could dilly down a rampaging bull
of a mugger with an erectile switchblade in a dark alley the
way Officer Netto could.

This time he had the accused on his arm, and the pair
approached the bench like a bride and groom. Mr. Honniger
looked brightly to left and right, taking everything in, smiling
in turn at the clerk, at Joel Avered, at the stenographer,
at the gaggle of court-watchers, and—most radiantly—at
the judge. Had such an arrestee ever been seen? He was a
white man. He had a full head of neatly brushed brown hair,
grizzled at the temples. He wore a tweed jacket and gray
flannel slacks, a shirt and a tie, and glistening brown loafers.
He was obviously not the least outraged by what was happening
to him.

"Samson Honniger, sir," Officer Netto said to the judge.

The judge was old Whinman, known as "the Whiner,"
famous for thinking that arraignment sessions—and prepositions—were wastes of everyone's time. He rattled off to Mr.
Honniger, with a speed that made the defendant shudder with
incomprehension, his rights—be represented an attorney, re-
main silent, if indigent public defender. It was as if the pressure
of the backlog of crimes on the court system had made of
Judge Whinman's larynx a kind of quick-operating trash com-
pactor. He now said, "What we got here?"

The clerk read the police report.

"Breaking entering larceny," the judge said. "Guilty not
guilty?"

"Not at all, Your Honor," Mr. Honniger serenely said.

"You had the damn dog your house," the judge said.

"The circumstances, sir, were not such that we could speak
of either breaking and entering or theft. I promise you."

"You want jury trial, judge trial?"

Mr. Honniger appeared to gaze into the depths of Judge Whinman's eyes, searching out the jurist's most private resources. Then, as if alarmed by what he saw, he took a step backward and hastily said, "Jury trial, if you please, sir."

"Remand trial. Felony charge. Bail a hundred."

That seemed to be the end of the matter. The clerk shouted the name of the next accused. Mr. Honniger looked shocked; he seemed to have counted on a much more impressive ceremony. Officer Netto took him by the hand and led him to the bail commissioner's desk, off to the right of the bench, and left him there. Joel watched the two men murmuring and saw the commissioner fill out a form and then point over at him in the jury box, indicating to Mr. Honniger the only bondsman in sight. Not permitted to approach the bail commissioner's desk, Joel stepped out of the jury box and waited for Mr. Honniger to come to him. Mr. Honniger handed him the form.

Joel glanced at it and said, "You must be here next Thursday morning at ten o'clock. Do you promise to come?"

"Oh, I look forward to it," Mr. Honniger said.

Joel told him that his bond had been set at one hundred dollars and that his bondsman's fee would be seven dollars; all would be forfeited, of course, if Mr. Honniger failed to appear.

"Fair enough," Mr. Honniger said.

"Are you good for that sum?"

"I don't happen to have that much on me."

"What can you put up?"

"Let me see." Mr. Honniger stepped into the jury box, sat down, bent forward, removed his shiny right shoe, took some bills from under an inner sole, counted out thirteen dollars, and offered them to Joel.

"Are you good for the rest? Can I trust you?"

Mr. Honniger had leaned over to put his shoe back on, so

Joel could not see his face, but he heard him say, "Cross my heart and hope to die."

There was a long silence. "All right," Joel finally said. "If you come next Thursday, you won't have to pay the rest. You'd better be here."

"I wouldn't miss it for anything."

At a little after eleven-thirty the following Thursday morning, the clerk announced the Honniger case, but the defendant did not come forward.

"Clerk call the bond," Judge Whinman ordered.

Alexander Cherevoy stood up and shouted, "Samson Honniger, appear in court or forfeit the bond in the amount of one hundred dollars."

Five seconds of silence. Then the judge: "What bondsman?"

"Avered," the clerk said.

"Not *again*," the judge vehemently said. "He here?"

Joel stood up in the jury box. "Here, sir."

"How much he post?"

"Thirteen dollars, Your Honor."

"How many times I warn you give too much credit?"

"It was all he had, sir."

"Necktie tweed coat all he had?"

"Yes, sir. Also, sir, the dog. The case interested me. Could we have a continuance, sir?"

"Get him. One week today."

"Thank you, Your Honor."

Joel had Samson Honniger's address, 23A Elm Street, on his copy of the bail commissioner's form, and as soon as court was recessed that afternoon he drove there. He rang the doorbell of the left half of a clapboarded double-occupancy house. Silence. He waited a long time, then rang again. Suddenly the door opened, and there stood Joel's client in what appeared to be a silk dressing gown, with a Paisley design, over pale gray pajamas. His hair was neatly brushed.

"Mr. Honniger," Joel said. He always called his clients Mr., Mrs., or Miss, no matter how old or young, how rich or poor. Or, if not using the name, he would say "sir," "ma'am," or "miss." He called a client's home "your residence," and he referred to the crimes they were accused of as "this unpleasantness they speak of" or "this little scrape we're in." He always shook hands with a client but never grasped the client's hand with both of his, and otherwise never touched a client, never on the arm, never on the shoulder, never in the small of the back. "Mr. Honniger," he now said, offering to shake hands. "You didn't keep your promise to me."

Mr. Honniger's handshake was vigorous. "Mr. Avered. I'm so glad to see you. Do come in. Please forgive my appearance. I was up very late last night."

Mr. Honniger led his guest into what he called his parlor —"Come into the parlor"—a small room that struck Joel as some sort of museum of oddities, or curio shop. Displayed on several tables—old-fashioned kitchen tables, with white enameled-metal tops—was an astonishing array of thinga-mabobs, doohickeys, knickknacks, gewgaws, and bits of flea-market bric-a-brac, arranged in rows and rows and rows. It took Joel's mind only a split second to ask itself, with an inner gasp of surprise, whether Mr. Honniger had stolen every one of these objects—whether, indeed, Mr. Honniger had been up very late the night before acquiring some more of these objects.

"Did I wake you up?" Joel asked.

"It doesn't matter at all," Mr. Honniger agreeably said. "It was high time to rise and shine."

"And do I take it that the reason you broke your promise to me is that you slept all morning?"

"My promise? . . . Oh my heavens, this was the morning I was supposed to be in court, wasn't it?"

"Yes, Mr. Honniger, it was. You're very fortunate. The judge agreed to a postponement."

"I'm sure I owe that to your kindness."

"I did request it. I have begun to wonder why I did. Mr. Honniger, tell me something. Why did you steal the dog?"

"I didn't break and enter, Mr. Avered, nor did I steal the dog. The door was unlocked, and the dog came away with me."

"Came away with you?"

"It was an affinity, Mr. Avered. Timothy understood me, and I understood Timothy. The moment we met. It was the strangest thing. His eyes reminded me of my grandmother's. The moment I looked in those brown eyes, I would have sworn—if I believed in reincarnation—I'd have sworn that behind those eyes was the mind of my Granny Sciseau. My maternal grandmother gave me my start in—"

"Please tell me about her another time," Joel said. "This is a busy day for me. You're telling me that you and this dog fell in love, and that he then simply insisted on going home with you?"

"I suppose one might think of it that way. It was Timothy's choice."

"How did you know the dog's name?"

"He was wearing a tag that said 'Call me Timothy.' "

"Did it ever cross your mind that the owners might miss Timothy?"

"Oh, yes, of course. But Timothy doesn't like them."

"How do you know?"

"Through the affinity I was speaking of."

"May I ask what kind of dog this is?"

"He is a Labrador. And a fine one. You know, the wide forehead of the best of that breed. Big chest. Straight tail. A fine dog."

"He must be. The owners put a valuation on him that made this little indiscretion of yours a felony."

It suddenly occurred to Joel that there had not been any prior-record notices in Mr. Honniger's court folder. "You've never been caught, sir," Joel said.

"I'm a careful man, Mr. Avered."

"But you were caught this time."

"I left a note for the owners. I didn't want them to worry."

"You gave them your name and address?"

"Of course. I had nothing to hide. As I say, this was Timothy's choice."

"Mr. Honniger, you're to appear next Thursday at ten. Kindly refrain from staying up late next Wednesday night."

"You're unusually kind, Mr. Avered. I don't want you to think I equate you with Timothy—with a dog, you know— but I might say I feel something like another affinity—"

"You're trying to get around me, Mr. Honniger. Just be there."

"Oh, yes, yes, yes, yes, yes, yes. I shall be there with bells on."

But Joel left with a heavy conviction that Mr. Honniger would forfeit his bond—all thirteen dollars of it.

And he did. On that next Thursday morning, Clerk Cherevoy once more called Samson Honniger's bond, and once more the defendant failed to present himself.

Joel Avered asked for a postponement.

Judge Whinman said, "Again? Not your life."

And now Joel realized he was one of the actors out there on the worn boards of the Pit, and he knew the time had come for him to join the judge in recital of certain time-honored formulas, the beauty of which (even when crunched in Judge Whinman's furiously hasty maw) seemed to him to help offset by a bit the pain of what had to be done.

JUDGE: "State obligation bring defendant speedy trial."

BONDSMAN: "Yes, Your Honor. I conclude that the said principal intends to abscond. I pray that a mittimus be issued."

JUDGE: "Hereby direct proper officer or indifferent person forthwith arrest—what's name?—Honniger—commit him jail until release due order law."

Alexander Cherevoy filled out the proper forms, and Joel Avered was thirteen dollars less poor than before.

At eight-thirty that evening, Joel rang the doorbell of a Georgian brick house on St. Alban Terrace. His heart was pounding. He was going to do something he had never done before—assume a false identity. He had felt an overwhelming need to meet Mr. Honniger's accuser. During the afternoon he had called a friend of his on the *Treehampstead Journal* to ask about Geoffrey Alford. His reporter friend had checked the paper's morgue and called back to say that the guy was a manufacturer of frozen grape-flavored lollipops who had apparently kicked up quite a little storm of money in two decades with this business. There were three separate clippings about lawsuits he had brought, one over a property-line dispute with a neighbor, one against an auto repair shop, and one contesting a relative's will. No, nothing about being a dog lover.

Mr. Alford answered the ring. "Yes?" he said, admitting Joel to the house but blocking his way beyond the front hall.

Joel introduced himself as the public defender assigned to Mr. Samson Honniger, whom Mr. Alford had alleged to have stolen his dog.

"So?"

Joel said he had come to see whether Mr. Alford intended to press his charge in court.

"You damn right I do," Mr. Alford said.

Joel saw that Mr. Alford's underjaw protruded—surely a genetic defect, but the fault had a characterological look about it—and he wore the facial expression of a man who had just made the mistake of tasting one of his Winepops, as his products were called. Joel saw bite sincerely written all over that face. "Timothy! Tim! Come! Come here!" Joel took a precautionary step backward.

Then he heard a groan and the tinkle of a chain collar and dog tags, and around the corner from the living room came lumbering a Labrador retriever, wagging its tail slowly but with enough scope so that its whole torso, and even its head, weaved back and forth with messages to Joel Avered of helpless amiability—but did Joel, under the influence of what his client had said, imagine that he saw the dog give his master a quite nasty look as he passed by him? Joel had had a Lab once, and he recognized the noble broad forehead of the old line of the breed, and the good wide chest. But Timothy's front legs were distinctly bowed, so he was shorter in front than in back, and at the outer bends of his forelegs he had the big callus pads of a being that slept away most of his days, his legs twitching and his tail thumping on the floor in unbearably sweet dreams of canned soybean meal and beef by-products.

Mr. Alford said, "Can you imagine a pervert that would want to steal *him?*"

Joel felt it his duty to say, "My client is not what I would call a pervert."

"The son of a bitch breaks in here—"

"Forgive me, sir. He didn't break in. He walked in. You should lock your doors."

"So he said in this goddamn note he leaves us. I never saw such a nerve."

"Did you keep the note, sir?"

"I sure did."

"Might I see it?"

"You stay right here," Mr. Alford said, with his underjaw stuck out even farther than usual. He went off to fetch the note.

Joel leaned over to pat Timothy, searching in his brown eyes for some signal from Mr. Honniger's Grandmother Sciseau, but the dog wheeled away to the side of the hall, crashed to the floor with another groan, and was sound asleep before Mr. Alford returned. Here he now came, reaching out a piece of paper in his right hand. "Read that," he said. "You won't believe this guy."

Joel read:

> *23A Elm Street,*
> *Treehampstead, Conn.*
>
> *Dear Host and Hostess:*
> *You have a charming house, with so many intriguing objets d'art on piano, coffee table, dining-room sideboard etc. that might tempt an intruder. I must therefore inform you that I was astonished to find your front door unlocked, and I would urge you to be more careful in the future.*
>
> *Sincerely yours,*
> *Samson Honniger*
> *P.S. Thank you for the dog.*

"Was anything missing," Joel asked, "aside from Timothy?"

"Isn't that enough? To steal a *dog?*"

"Timothy doesn't seem to be any worse off for the experience. Do you really feel a need to go to trial?"

"He sure as hell is worse off. He won't eat. I think the bastard poisoned him."

Samson Honniger was rearrested, and this time the judge set bail at one thousand dollars and warned Avered that if he gave the accused a single dollar of credit he would bar him from further business in the Fifth Circuit Court. In order to scare up money for the bond, Mr. Honniger took Joel with him, first to his house and then to Fanter's Pawn Shop, downtown, where tickets on just three tiny items from one of Mr. Honniger's parlor tables netted him enough for his bail.

"Johnny Fanter has a wonderful eye for value," Mr. Honniger said as they left the pawnshop.

"He seemed to know you quite well," Joel said.

"He's a good judge of character," Mr. Honniger said. "He trusts me."

Seated as usual in the jury box, one morning about a fortnight before the day set for Mr. Honniger's trial, Joel was astonished to see Mr. Honniger's name on the arrest list again. And there it said again in so many words: ". . . theft of dog."

Judge Whinman's eyebrows did a little dance when he saw Samson Honniger come smiling up the aisle again on Nelly Netto's arm. "Same dog, different dog?" the judge asked.

"Your Honor, sir," Mr. Honniger said, "I was out all evening, and when I came home very late, Timothy was sleeping on my front porch."

"You claim you never went owner's house?"

"I'll wager, sir, that if you took the trouble to inspect the owner's home, you'd find a front-door screen broken out—something of the sort. Timothy wanted to be with me."

There was a slight ripple of conversation and laughter from the area of the court-watchers' folding chairs.

At this moment the case of the stolen dog seemed to have reached the outer edge of Judge Whinman's juridical patience. "Quiet!" he roared, suddenly so upset that he broke out with several distinct prepositions. "If you want to talk, I'll put you in the cellblock for the morning. If you don't believe me, try me. This facility is bad enough without the conduct on top of it." Then he turned to the clerk and said in more normal tones, "When this person stand trial?"

As Alexander Cherevoy started riffling through papers, Joel said from the jury box, "On the thirteenth, Your Honor."

"That you, Avered? You get full amount bail last time?"

"Yes, sir. Every cent."

"Remove him."

During *voir dire* of jurors on the morning of the trial, Winthrop Clacks, the public defender assigned to Mr. Honniger, shook his head and muttered to Joel, "I wouldn't have half of these characters to try my dog."

This remark touched a nerve in Joel, because it seemed to him that what was really to be tested in this trial was the soul of Timothy, the Labrador retriever.

The very first thing that morning, after having asked what was coming up in this session, Judge Whinman had said, "I want the dog here." This had caused a conference between Clerk Cherevoy and Bailiff Esposito, out in the middle of the floor—a chat that gave to those two their usual function of setting the day's tone. There was an air of heavy doubt about their murmuring. An animal witness? Was the Fifth Circuit Court in danger of becoming a circus? Had the Honorable Eustace Whinman mislaid, as these two evidently had long feared he might, his marbles? Bailiff Esposito went off to make some phone calls. He was gone some time. On his return, he reported to the clerk. The clerk shook his head, with the slow stretching movement back and forth of one in whom incredulity causes severe neck pain.

Then Alexander Cherevoy said in a loud voice, "Your Honor, it will be necessary for you to make a call to the City Animal Officer."

The judge naturally wanted to know why.

"The dog is in the pound. It bit its master last night."

And so, Joel thought, hearing the official scorn of the clerk's voice pronouncing those words, yes, the soul of an allegedly criminal animal *would* be put in the balance this time. Was such a soul entitled, in this temple of justice, to affinities— and to violent antipathies? To feelings so vivid and seductive and corrosive as to seduce human beings into indecent acts— felony, litigious revenge, and, yes, the carrying out of a cruel and unusual punishment, the arbitrary sentencing of a beast, without trial, to incarceration in a pound? Would the Final Judge make choices of value among the species of the living? Could dogs be among His elect—and His damned? Could a creature capable of wagging its entire body as a signal of peaceful intention have been born with the curse of original sin?

The jury was chosen with uncommon speed; neither attorney used any peremptory challenges. By about eleven-thirty the panel had been sworn, and the complainant entered the room wearing a world-class scowl and with white bandages wrapped bulkily around his right hand. He was accompanied by an attorney from Winthrop, Thrull & Panstrom. The pair stood at the table in front of the bench, and the clerk called out, "Alford versus Honniger."

As the prosecutor stepped forward to elucidate the charge to the jury, Judge Whinman growled, "Make it short sweet."

The prosecutor in that month was Romeo Orp, who hated everything soft in the American system of justice that might ease the levies on the lawless—loathed bail, loathed probation, loathed continuances, loathed paroles, loathed public defenders and lenient judges. Joel had often thought that a man so riddled with hatreds would harbor a bleeding ulcer; no such thing. Prosecutor Orp was always in the pink of good cheer. He belabored the accused with the natural grace of an athlete playing—and confident of winning—a contact sport. He was, this morning, indeed brief, because his contempt for a person who could steal a dog was so great as to make the case appear to him proven by the mere act of describing it in three sentences.

Mr. Clacks, the public defender, wasted no words, either. His motive for brevity was indifference, for he, as the saying went, could care less. He said, "Man says he didn't steal the dog, the dog just followed him home."

"All right," Judge Whinman said. "I want the defendant stand right over here. Face the jury box. Now, the complainant down there other end, other side the bailiff's desk, far as you can get. Face the jury. You ready? . . . Esposito, let's have the dog. Leave him loose. Don't use no leash."

The bailiff disappeared through the lockup door, which clanged shut behind him. Soon the door opened again, and out came Timothy. Joel, seated in the onlooker's section now that the jury box was occupied, could see that the black dog was in no hurry to settle a case at law. It sniffed its way to the jury box, then toward the bench, looked up piercingly for a moment into the judge's eyes—just as Samson Honniger had done on that first day, Joel recalled—and, without a flicker of concern or respect, put his nose down again and ranged around the room savoring the spoor of countless lost souls. It seemed to Joel that Timothy knew he was in charge, and that he wanted to spend a few minutes devoting his keenest sense to a study of human folly. Joel suddenly remembered, from way back in elementary school, the goose pimples he'd got when a friend had pointed out to him that "God" was just "dog" backward. There was an awesome hush in the courtroom.

Then the spell broke. Lifting his head high, Timothy took one sharp look around and made for Samson Honniger. During this trip his tail described circles of ecstasy. He sat straight in front of the defendant, his tail now sweeping back and forth on the floor and kicking up a little cloud of dust.

There was a flurry of conversation in the jury box. Then the foreman arose and said, "Your Honor, could we try that again? Could we have the two men over on this side of the room, facing away from us, and try again?"

"What for?" the judge said.

"We only had a rear view of the dog when it went over there. We want to see it front on when it decides."

So Bailiff Esposito took Timothy to the lockup, Alford and Honniger moved to the other side of the room and turned around, and the dog was let in again. Joel thought for a moment that in view of Timothy's power, in these circumstances, to make a shrewd comment on ambiguities in human justice of sorts he had experienced all his life, the dog might this time go and sit with his tail thrashing in front of his master. But he did not. He went around sniffing again, as if he had never been in the place before, and then, once again, danced over to Samson Honniger and sat facing him.

"You satisfied?" the judge asked the jurors.

The foreman stood and said, "Yes, sir, Your Honor. We've seen enough."

The judge asked the bailiff to lead the twelve to the jury room. They deliberated for exactly four minutes and sent word out that they had arrived at a verdict. When they had filed back into the jury box, the clerk shouted: "Does the jury find the defendant guilty as charged, or not guilty?"

The foreman said, "Guilty."

The judge said, "How come guilty? The damn dog chose the defendant."

"Yes, sir," the foreman said. "But. The eyes were the thing. We didn't like the way the man and the dog looked at each other. One of the jurors used the word 'mischief,' something between those two. But the rest of us thought it was worse than that, Your Honor, that the man is not just a thief—we could see *that* plain as a deuce of spades, you better search his house—but more than that, there's a lot of dog in him, there really is, underneath all those clean clothes and that smiling. One of our jurors said that you had to lay it on the line and say he's a son of a bitch. But the dog's eyes were the limit, sir. It clinched it, when we reversed things. That dog is a troublemaker. I'm not telling Your Honor any news when I say it takes a crook to know a crook. We didn't like what went on between those two. They're both guilty—theft, confidence game, alienation of affection, desertion, assault, you name it, sir."

Judge Whinman turned to the complainant. "Whatsyourname," he said. "Alford. Want the dog back?"

Mr. Alford held up his bandaged hand. "You think I'm crazy?"

"All right," the judge said. "I sentence you—whatsyourname—Honniger, take care the damn dog until it dies or you die, whichever is sooner."

Joel then saw a look of utter dismay spread on Samson Honniger's face. A few minutes later, Joel peeled off nine one-hundred-dollar bills and three tens—bail minus fee—and laid them on the free man's palm. Then he said, "Timothy won't like your going out late at night, Mr. Honniger."

Mr. Honniger, aplomb fully restored, shot his lower jaw out toward the dog for a moment, mimicking the Alford underbite. Timothy growled but also wagged his tail. "Thank you for trusting me, Mr. Avered," Mr. Honniger said, and he left the courtroom through the public door, snapping the thumb and third finger of his left hand to bring Timothy to heel.

John Hersey was born in Tientsin, China, in 1914 and lived there until 1925, when his family returned to the United States. He studied at Yale and Cambridge universities, served for a time as Sinclair Lewis's secretary, and then worked several years as a journalist. He has had published fourteen books of fiction and eight books of reportage and essays, and has won the Pulitzer Prize for fiction. He divides his time between Key West and Martha's Vineyard. He is married and has five children and four grandchildren.

A NOTE ON THE TYPE

The text of this book was set in a film version of Garamond No. 3, a modern rendering of the type first cut
by Claude Garamond (1510–1561). Garamond was a
pupil of Geoffroy Troy and is believed to have based his
letters on Venetian models, although he introduced a
number of important differences, and it is to him we
owe the letter which we know as old style. He gave to
his letters a certain elegance and a feeling of movement
that won for their creator an immediate reputation and
the patronage of Francis I of France.

Composed by Crane Typesetting Service, Inc.
West Barnstable, Massachusetts

Printed and bound by The Haddon Craftsmen, Inc.,
Scranton, Pennsylvania

Typography and binding design
by Dorothy S. Baker